"Get down!" Steve lurched at Joss. She whirled to face him. "Down! Sniper in the trees."

She dropped beside the bed. He fell at her side. A bullet smashed through the window.

"Stay here!" Steve told her. "I'm going after him."

"Steve!"

"I have to go now, Joss. While we know where the sniper is. Call 911. Tell them what's happened and don't hang up until backup arrives."

He fled down the steps and ran out the back door, letting it bang closed behind him. Steve raced toward the edge of the property. The shooter had come from beyond the metal toolshed. Possibly in a tree, as he'd hit the second-floor window.

The pager hooked to his belt sprang to life. The dispatcher issued an active-shooting announcement, then she proceeded to spit out a call for police backup to Joss's address. Within moments, Steve knew, the road would be barricaded and police would swarm the area. No one underestimated the danger of a shooter on the loose.

Was this the same man who'd shot Linda, or was there yet another shooter out there intent on ending Joss's life?

Dana R. Lynn grew up in Illinois. She met her husband at a wedding and told her parents she'd met the man she was going to marry. Nineteen months later, they were married. Today, they live in rural Pennsylvania with their three children and a variety of animals. In addition to writing, she works as a teacher for the deaf and hard of hearing and is active in her church.

Books by Dana R. Lynn

Love Inspired Suspense

Amish Country Justice

Plain Target
Plain Retribution
Amish Christmas Abduction
Amish Country Ambush
Amish Christmas Emergency
Guarding the Amish Midwife
Hidden in Amish Country
Plain Refuge
Deadly Amish Reunion
Amish Country Threats
Covert Amish Investigation
Amish Christmas Escape
Amish Cradle Conspiracy
Her Secret Amish Past

Visit the Author Profile page at LoveInspired.com.

HER SECRET
AMISH PAST

DANA R. LYNN

LOVE INSPIRED SUSPENSE
INSPIRATIONAL ROMANCE

LOVE INSPIRED® SUSPENSE

INSPIRATIONAL ROMANCE

ISBN-13: 978-1-335-58823-4

Recycling programs
for this product may
not exist in your area.

Her Secret Amish Past

For questions and comments about the quality of this book, please contact us at CustomerService@Harlequin.com.

Love Inspired
22 Adelaide St. West, 41st Floor
Toronto, Ontario M5H 4E3, Canada
www.LoveInspired.com

Printed in U.S.A.

Thou art my hiding place and my shield: I hope in thy word.
—*Psalm* 119:114

For Virginia. More than family,
you were a friend and a constant encourager.
I will miss you. See you on the other side.

ONE

I KNOW WHO YOU ARE.

Josslyn Graham plucked the note from under the windshield wipers on her mother's car and frowned. She turned it to see the other side. Only one line, typed in large block letters, disturbed the crisp whiteness of the standard copy paper. What did it mean?

Squinting against the afternoon sun glinting off the fresh January snow, she glanced around, searching for the person who left the note. When had it been left? The note hadn't been there half an hour ago when she'd arrived home from work. Of course, it had been snowing on and off all day. Now, there was nothing suspicious in sight. All she saw was the thick line of pine trees surrounding the house. She didn't even see footsteps, thanks to the constant precipitation.

A drop of icy wetness hit her cheek. Then another. It was beginning to snow again. A feathery flake drifted onto the paper and melted. She held the note closer to her body, protecting it from the weather.

Her mother stepped outside of the house and locked the door. Turning with a smile at her daughter, she held tight to the railing and descended the stairs. She walked to Joss, her fur-lined boots crunching on the snow packed on the driveway. It was time to plow again. By the time she reached her daughter, tiny snowflakes covered her salt-and-pepper hair.

"We had better hurry. We won't have time for dinner before the show if we don't get a move on. It's already a quarter to one, and the show starts at seven. I can't believe we're leaving so late."

Joss smiled at her mother. For Christmas, she'd given her tickets to see a play at the local theater. They planned to hit a couple of shops, then eat dinner and go to the performance. "We've got time. Relax."

"It's a good thing the doctor's office closes early on Wednesdays, and that you were free. I know you don't like to take time off." She pointed at the paper in Joss's hand. "What's that? Did you make a list?"

Joss shook her head. Something in her hesitated to show her mother. But the note was on Linda Graham's car. "No. This was tucked under your wipers."

She handed the note to her mother.

Linda glanced at it. Her smile melted away and the letter fell from her hands. Her eyes bulged. The color drained from her face, leaving her pale and shaking. When she swayed, Joss hurried over and took her arm.

"Mom? Mom! What's going on? What does it mean? Are you okay? Should we call the police?"

"No! No police. We have to go now."

Joss opened her mouth, intending to insist they call law enforcement. Something stopped her. She'd never seen her mother so freaked out. Sheer terror glazed her familiar eyes. Joss shivered. Maybe she should wait until her mother had calmed down. Once she got the whole story, she could go to the police if it was necessary. Her mom was her priority now.

Linda turned to her daughter and clutched at her arms. "Jossie, we have to go!"

"I know, Mom. I'm just waiting for you—"

"No!" Linda's fingers tensed on her arm. "Forget the play. We must go now, and we can't come back. Quickly! Pack a bag. Only take what is essential. We'll leave the rest behind."

Shocked, Joss stared. She'd never seen her mother this frantic.

"Not coming back? Mom, I don't understand. What's going on?" Fresh goose bumps arose.

Linda broke away from her and ran back to the house, grabbing the railing so she wouldn't slip on the fresh snow glazing the wooden steps.

"Don't ask me! There's no time. I'll explain in the car."

"What about my job? Mom?"

Linda waved away the question. "They can get a new receptionist. You have to trust me."

The door slammed shut behind Linda, giving Joss no chance to respond.

She could refuse to go. After all, it wasn't like she was a minor. She'd turned twenty-five last month. If she really wanted, she could dig in her heels and stay behind. And what? Forever wonder where her mom was, or if she was okay?

Bending down, she picked up the paper that had prompted her mother's reaction. The words popped out at her. *I KNOW WHO YOU ARE.* She glanced back to the house. It was obvious her mother had secrets. Thinking back, Joss recalled starting school in a new city every year until they moved here. Every June, like clockwork, they'd pack up their belongings and move. When she'd ask why, there was always a reason. A better job, more opportunities, better climate for Joss's health. Joss had lived in Illinois, Iowa, Kentucky, Virginia and Pennsylvania before they'd finally landed in Sutter Springs, Ohio, just in time for Joss to begin her sophomore year in high school. That was ten years ago. They'd lived in this small house on the outskirts of town ever since.

She took in the familiar house, with its reddish-brown log cabin siding, the privacy line of trees and the familiar two-tenths of a mile-long driveway that was barely visible from the road. She'd always thought her mom had loved the quiet and the charm of the small home.

Suddenly, she saw it with different eyes. What if this wasn't just a comfortable home? Maybe it was some kind of safe house. The idea would have seemed ridiculous an hour ago, but now? Now, things she'd never questioned appeared suspicious.

Things like the multiple moves they'd made while she was growing up.

Had her mother been running all this time, hiding under the guise of searching out new opportunities? Joss shivered, but not from the icy wind buffeting her cheeks until they were numb.

Why had she accepted it each time they'd picked up and relocated?

Fueled by her mother's desperation and fear, she bolted up the steps and into the house. Drawers opening and closing followed by rapid footsteps sounded in her mother's room. Joss imagined Linda was running back and forth between her dresser and bed.

Joss ducked into her own room. Pictures plastered the walls, mostly snapshots she'd taken. She hesitated. No. Whatever was happening, she didn't have time to waste. She hoped she'd get the story from her anxious parent, and they'd figure out what to do. There was no question in her mind about the chances of them returning home.

If only she knew who or what they were running from.

Grabbing her suitcase out of the closet, Joss stuffed the essentials into the bag. She stopped short at the books lining her bookshelves. Her throat ached. Those books were old friends, some of them read multiple times. They were all she'd had growing up because she had known better than to let herself get too attached to anyone.

She didn't belong anywhere.

Except, she'd let her guard down in the past

few years. Allowed herself to be lulled into believing the days of leaving at a moment's notice were over.

Pain hit her stomach. She doubled over, crossing her arms across her middle. She couldn't do it, couldn't abandon everything. Straightening against the pain, she set her shoulders. In a moment of defiance, she grabbed a second bag and crammed her favorite books, her Bible and her journal inside, together with her collection of highlighters and gel pens. She might have to leave, at least for the moment, but she'd bring as much with her as she could.

"Joss! Let's go! Now!"

Sighing, she grabbed her bags then half ran out to the car. Her mom was already shoving her suitcase into it. Joss let the door clang shut behind her and hurried to the vehicle. Although her mother gave her a sharp glance when she spied the extra bag, she didn't take the time to scold.

Closing the trunk, Joss jogged around to the passenger side of the twelve-year-old four-door sedan her mother drove and got in. Had she grabbed the note from off her bed? She had meant to put it into the back with her journal so she could show it to the police later. She was pretty sure it was in the bag. No time to check now. Her mom revved the engine. One look at her mom's expression told Joss that Linda Graham was not in the mood to wait until Joss checked her bags. Joss buckled her seat belt. She stifled a gasp when her normally cautious parent hastily backed up, spinning the steering wheel so the car swung in a wide arc. After a quick glance in each direction, Linda sped down the narrow driveway. When the car arrived at the end, she barely stopped before barreling out onto the road.

"Mom! These roads are slick. Take it easy." Wherever they were heading, she wanted to arrive in one piece.

"We're fine." Linda's mouth was a straight, tense line slashed across her face. "They've been plowed, and we have snow tires. We can't risk being too slow. They're coming."

Joss took a deep breath and closed her eyes. This was not how she'd planned to spend her day. Tears gathered, threatening to leak and pour down her face, but she blinked them back. She couldn't break down. Not yet. She needed to know who was after them and why.

"Mom. Don't you think we're overreacting? Who would warn us if they planned on coming after us? It doesn't make sense."

Linda frowned. "No, it doesn't. And warning us wouldn't be his style. He'd be stealthy and corner us. Still, we can't take the chance. I was a fool to stay in one place for so long. I let my guard down."

Joss's stomach clenched. "Who? I have no idea what you are talking about. Who would come after us?"

Linda met her eyes, then jerked her gaze away. Joss shivered at the despair in them. "Not now. Please, Joss, it's really complicated. Now is not the time."

Joss's world wobbled a little farther off its axis. For whatever reason, someone was after them and her mother knew why. She recalled her mother's refusal to call the police. "Are you in trouble with the law? Have you done something illegal?"

Linda laughed, a harsh, bitter sound. One that hit her heart like hard pebbles.

"There was wrong done, but not by me. At least not intentionally." Her mother shook her head. "Later, Joss. Please."

Nodding, Joss settled back into her seat, holding tight to a grab handle as the car zoomed down the road at an impossible speed. How was it possible that she didn't know this about her own mother? Suddenly, the woman behind the steering wheel seemed like a stranger to her.

The scenery passed by in a blur of white. Ice coated the branches. Normally, she would have taken the time to grab her camera and snap photos while she admired their beauty, the way they seemed as if they were made of crystal.

Her mom opened her mouth. A roar behind them made Joss glance over her shoulder. A large SUV was gaining on them. It swerved to the other lane to pass. As it drove by, she glanced over and into the cold, dark eyes of the driver. For a single, frozen moment, she stared into his face. He raised his arm.

She screamed. "He has a gun!"

He opened fire. Linda jerked the wheel to the right. Bullets peppered the side of the car and shattered the windows. The car slid off the road, slammed into the edge of the guardrail and flipped over before sliding down the embankment toward the tree looming in its path.

Slam!

When the motion stopped, Joss turned, opened her eyes and shuddered. The car had stopped at an odd angle, so she was looking down at the mangled front windshield. Her stomach lurched. The airbags had not deployed, probably because the vehicle was so old, and her mother had been less than vigilant about maintenance. Ignoring the searing pain slashing through her head and neck, she turned to look at her mother.

"Mom!"

Linda's head hung limply. Blood plopped onto the steering wheel in large droplets. Joss struggled to release her seat belt so she could assist her mother. It clicked, and she fell forward, banging her head on the dashboard.

"Mom."

Her mother didn't respond. Joss's forehead throbbed. She leaned toward her mom. Before she could touch her, a wave of dizziness washed over her. White noise bloomed in her head. She fought against it, even as she fell back in her seat and lost consciousness.

"All units. Shots fired on West Willow Avenue."

Sergeant Steve Beck listened to the dispatcher's voice coming through the radio, frowning. He was minutes away from the location. It was a sparsely populated residential area. He hit the button on his radio and responded to the call. After he disconnected with dispatch, he flipped on his Sutter Springs Police Department cruiser's lights and siren.

Steve glanced around. There was no other traffic on the road, so he executed a precise

U-turn and headed away from town. A large SUV sped past his cruiser, whipping up a cloud of snow and dust in its wake. Steve slowed, his hands tightening on the wheel, unable to see the road ahead of him through the whiteout conditions. When the air cleared, he surged forward.

He needed to get to the scene, but he couldn't ignore someone driving so recklessly.

Punching in the button to connect him to dispatch, he waited until someone answered. When the dispatcher at central picked up, he kept it brief.

"Hey, Leslie. Sergeant Beck here. A large blue SUV heading south on West Willow Avenue just went by me, exceeding the speed limit and driving dangerously. I'm unsure if the driver was involved in the shooting. I will be on location in under two minutes."

"Understood, Sergeant."

He approached a blind curve and tapped his brakes to slow his cruiser, hugging the outside edge of the road to avoid colliding with any oncoming vehicles. Coming out of the twist, he sucked in a hard breath. There was no sign of a shooter. Instead, he noticed the edge of the guardrail was a buckled, mangled mess, strangely flattened as if an enormous weight had crushed it.

An enormous weight like a car flipping and rolling over it.

He'd seen this before. Clenching his jaw, he fought back the memories of the wreck that had taken everything from him. Someone needed his help. Now was not the time to get bogged down with painful recollections.

Later, much later, he'd think about it.

He swerved over to the narrow strip beside the snow-covered blacktop. The moment his cruiser rolled to a stop, he jumped from the cruiser and hurried over to peer down the slope. The car below was nearly as mangled as the guardrail. He ran back to the cruiser and contacted dispatch again, calling for backup, an ambulance and the volunteer fire department.

"Tell them they might need the Jaws of Life."

"Yes, Sergeant," Leslie replied briskly. "I'm putting the request in now."

He hung up, satisfied. Leslie was as efficient as they came. Now he had to wait, and that could be another issue. It would take at least six or seven minutes for anyone to arrive. And that was if any of the local volunteer firefighters were available to take the call. Most of the firefighters had full-time jobs. If no one responded, the dispatcher would have to widen the call to the nearby departments.

It was up to him. Gathering his jacket, hat and gloves, he left the warmth of his vehicle and jogged to his trunk. He wouldn't be able to bring too much along, but he grabbed a first aid kit, an insulated blanket and a flashlight. He might not accomplish much alone, but at least he could try to keep anyone injured warm and ward off the onset of shock.

Approaching the end of the ruined guardrail, he paused. Was that a shell casing? Crouching down, he peered closer. It was. It looked like a .38. He'd found the scene of the shooting. He quickly snapped a photo of it on his phone and then pulled an evidence bag out of his car and collected it. This time, he used his phone to call for the Crime Scene Unit. He couldn't process a scene and deal with possible injuries at the same time. His gaze retuned to the crashed vehicle on the shoulder, down an embankment, and rushed to it.

Slipping and sliding down the steep hill, he caught the door handle to halt his forward trek. One glance in the driver's side window told him the driver had sustained serious injuries. Blood coated her hair and the steering wheel. Beyond her, a second woman sprawled between the seat and the floorboard. Somehow, she'd gotten her seat belt unfastened.

He didn't see any blood on her, but she wasn't moving either. Although the hood of the car had caved in from the force of the impact, it didn't appear either woman was trapped. If he could get the doors open, they wouldn't need the Jaws of Life.

He grabbed the door handle and tugged. Nothing. He hadn't expected it to budge, but he'd hoped. Next, he pounded on the window. The driver didn't even twitch. The passenger, however, lifted her head and gave him a bleary glance. She blinked twice at him, and the fog cleared out of her light brown eyes.

"Can you unlock the doors?" he shouted and pointed to the door panel. Her forehead wrinkled.

He hollered his request again.

She straightened and nodded once. Reaching behind her, she hit the unlock button on her side of the car. The sharp click of the mechanism seemed loud in the still winter air. Without hesitation, Steve grabbed the handle and opened the door. He removed his glove and searched the driver for a pulse with bare fingers.

There. It was faint, but she was still alive.

"My mom, is she still…" the younger woman asked, her voice quavering.

Her mom. He swallowed the thick sympathy

welling inside his throat. He of all people understood the agony of this moment.

"Yes, she's alive. I've called for help. I don't want to release her myself."

She nodded, then winced. "She might have back or neck injuries."

Her words came out slightly garbled, as if she was speaking around a mouthful of marbles. Steve narrowed his eyes and focused on her, trying to see if she was just emotional or if shock was setting in. The interior of the car was too deep in shadows for any certainty.

"Ma'am, I'm Sergeant Steve Beck. I won't leave you. Just hang on, okay? Help will be here soon. We'll get you and your mama out."

That's all he could promise. As much as he'd like to, there was no way he could assure her that either she or her mother would be all right.

"What's your name?"

"Joss. Josslyn Graham. My mom's name is Linda."

The siren of an emergency vehicle nearing drew his attention back to the road. An ambulance pulled behind his cruiser, followed by a second cruiser. A fire truck siren blared in the distance.

"Help has arrived, Miss Graham."

Steve stepped back to let the experts go

to work as they gathered around the injured women in the car. He should go assist with traffic control. It took longer to ascend the embankment, slippery with snow, than it did coming down. Finally, he made it up.

The afternoon light was fading when the first stretcher carrying the mother reached the top of the embankment. Her waxy complexion worried him. Cole, the lead paramedic, looked at him.

"Is she going to make it?" Steve kept his voice low, even though he knew the daughter was still down below.

"I wish I knew. She's been shot, Steve." Cole leaned closer to him. "The bullet went into her shoulder, and she's lost a lot of blood. I can't tell if it nicked an artery. She needs surgery, STAT."

Steve clenched his teeth, remembering the bullet casing he'd discovered. "I'm going to turn this over to the CSU when they get on scene. Then I'll go to the hospital. I'm hoping the daughter will be lucid and walk me through what happened. She didn't appear to be injured as seriously as the mother."

It sounded cold and unfeeling. It was also only partially the truth. Yes, he wanted to question her. Beyond that, though, he wanted to be there until someone she knew got to the hospital. No one should face the possible death of a loved one alone. Not like he'd been...

He twisted his mind away from the thought of his family's destruction.

A few minutes later, the second stretcher carrying the daughter arrived. She was conscious when she reached the second ambulance. Her wild eyes searched until they landed on Steve. "My mom..."

"Go with them, Miss Graham. I'll be coming to the hospital as soon as I can."

For some reason, his assurance calmed her.

He didn't want to dwell on that.

Cole tossed a brisk wave and climbed behind the wheel. Steve watched the ambulance pull out onto the road, then slid into his cruiser and called his superior officer, Chief Mike Spencer.

"What can you tell me, Sergeant?"

"Not much, sir. The only vehicle on scene contained two women, both of whom are on the way to Sutter Springs Memorial Hospital as we speak. A mother and daughter." The Crime Scene Unit approached from the opposite direction. He waved at them, holding up a finger to let them know he'd be right there. "The mom's in really bad shape. I found one casing at the scene, but due to the situation, I am letting the CSU handle it and heading to the hospital ASAP. They're here now."

"Good call. Keep me posted."

He hung up and jumped out of the car. The quicker he explained the situation, the sooner he'd be on his way.

Twenty minutes later, he parked his cruiser in the hospital parking lot and made his way inside the hospital. The receptionist smiled politely as he strolled up to the reception area and leaned his elbows on the counter.

"May I help you, Officer?"

"Sergeant Beck, ma'am. Two women injured in a drive-by shooting were brought in."

She shook her head slowly, making a tsking sound. "Yes, Josslyn Graham and her mother, Linda. Joss is a receptionist at the pediatrician's office. Such a shock!"

He waited for her to point the way.

"They're both in the emergency room. I'll buzz you in."

"Thank you."

The emergency room bustled with activity. Doctors, nurses and other hospital staff rushed in every direction. He snagged a nurse's attention. She pointed him in the correct direction.

Arriving at the cubicle, he called out and a feminine voice told him to enter. It was the young woman from the crash. Two dark bruises marred her pretty face, one on her forehead and the other on her right cheek. She was sitting on the narrow hospital bed, her legs hanging over the edge.

"Have you heard anything about my mom?" she begged.

"Not yet, Miss Graham."

"Joss," she corrected him.

"Joss, I'll find out what I can about your mom, but I need to ask you what happened."

Her glittering brown eyes flattened and grew shuttered at his words.

He opened his mouth to interrogate her further but was interrupted by the curtain rustling as a doctor entered.

"Miss Graham, do you happen to know your blood type? Your mother lost a lot of blood."

Her face paled. Steve shifted closer so he could catch her if she fainted. Her eyes flicked to him briefly.

"I do. I give blood quarterly. I'm type O."

The doctor's mouth dropped open briefly, then closed with a click. "I see. I didn't realize... Are you adopted?"

Her eyes flared wide. "N-no."

Even Steve could hear the uncertainty.

The doctor hesitated. "It's very rare for an AB mother to have a child with blood type O."

"Maybe my father was an O?"

"Still very rare."

The silence was thick with fear and unanswered questions.

After several moments, Joss lifted her head. "Are you telling me that Linda Graham is not my mother?"

Red flags went off in his mind. He'd heard of parents deciding not to inform their children they were adopted. He wasn't qualified to judge whether they were right or wrong. However, when that parent and adult child were the victims in a drive-by shooting, the time for privacy was over. He had a shooter to apprehend, which meant he needed answers, and he needed them now.

TWO

Who was she? Was she really Josslyn Graham, the daughter of Linda Graham?

Another thought edged its way into the chaos filling her mind. The note had claimed to know who her mother was. Several possibilities floated around in her head, but she couldn't sort through them now. Not while the shock was still fresh. She needed to focus on the present.

The questions continued to rise to the surface and swim around in her mind. Who was she and who was Linda Graham? How much of her life had been a fabrication? And was this why they'd never remained in one place too long?

Joss stared at the doctor, waiting for him to deny it, to reassure her that all was well and that her mother hadn't lied her entire life. Or at least give her some clue as to how this could have all happened.

Instead, he lowered his head and peered at her over his wire-rimmed glasses. Compassion simmered in his gaze. "I apologize for unsettling you. I never would have said anything if I thought you didn't know. Your mother's situation, however, is grave. Our blood bank is dangerously low, and she's lost a lot of blood. While not a match, type O can be given to a person with type AB."

A hand touched her elbow. She jumped. It was the cop. She'd forgotten he was there.

"I know you're confused." His deep voice washed over her. "Let's worry about your mother, then we'll deal with the other stuff."

Joss blinked at him, working to think beyond the fog clouding her mind. She wanted to cry at his understatement. Confused? That didn't cover her emotions. She couldn't even sort them all out. Then she thought of the rest of his statement, about dealing with her mother first. He was right. She nodded, accepting the plan. It was a place to start.

The doctor pulled back the curtain surrounding them. He ducked his head out of the emergency room cubicle and called for a nurse. The rest of the instructions flew by. It didn't matter. She had worked in a medical office long enough to know the drill. A moment later a nurse bustled in, her skid-resistant shoes making a soft shuffling sound. The sharp scent of alcohol hit her nose seconds before the nurse swabbed her arm and began searching for a good vein.

Her stomach twisted when she saw the needle. She gave blood because she wanted to save lives. That didn't mean she enjoyed feeling like a pincushion. *Breathe through your nose. Don't pass out.*

She settled herself against the thin, starchy pillow and looked away. The needle pierced her skin. Wincing, she focused on the cop. What was his name again? Beck. Sergeant Beck. She couldn't recall his first name. She knew he had numerous questions regarding the accident.

Her breath stuttered in her chest at the memory of the man who'd done this to them.

He'd shot her mother. As if it they were nothing, he'd aimed that gun at them and pulled the trigger.

"Miss Graham? Are you all right?"

The deep voice pulled her back. Lifting her eyelids, she gazed at the cop, now standing directly beside her, frowning.

Flushing, she looked away and noticed the nurse had completed taking blood. That was quick. With an impersonal smile, the nurse pressed a cotton ball to the puncture and put a bandage over it to hold it in place.

"All set." The efficient nurse gathered her supplies and whisked out of the cubicle, leaving Joss alone with Sergeant Beck. Reclining on a hospital bed while a stranger watched was an uncomfortable feeling. Joss leaned forward, intending to sit on the edge of the bed again, and immediately regretted her action. Wooziness took her by surprise. The room swam around her.

"Whoa, there!" Strong arms caught her before she tipped over the side of the narrow surface. "You should take it easy for a few minutes. Maybe have some juice. Here."

A paper cup nudged her fingers. Embarrassed, she grasped for the orange juice and quickly downed the sweet beverage, wrinkling her nose slightly at the taste. She knew better than to move so soon. She was always woozy after giving blood. Her fingers trembled as she handed the empty cup to him.

"Thanks." Sighing, she met his eyes. "And thanks for earlier. I think you saved our lives."

At the mention of why they'd met, he stepped away to a professional distance. "You're welcome. Can you tell me what happened?"

Where to start? Her stomach clenched. Resting her elbows on her thighs, she hunched over, head in her hands, and closed her eyes. Pain and sorrow dug in as she recalled their plans that morning. The day had been such a normal day, full of promise and expectation. Until…

She jolted upright, grabbing the edge of the bed to hold herself steady. "We got a note. That's what started this."

"A note?"

She nodded. "Uh-huh. It was typed in block letters. 'I know who you are,' it said."

Sergeant Beck's forehead creased. "Any idea who could have written it? Or what it meant?"

"No idea. Although, I think it's obvious my mom's been keeping secrets from me."

A lot of secrets, some of them potentially deadly.

Sergeant Beck's eyes narrowed. Not in a suspicious what-are-you-hiding way, but in a thoughtful manner. "I need to see this note. Is it with you?"

Memories of the events leading to the current crisis washed over her like a tidal wave. Joss ducked her head and squeezed her lids shut, striving to hold the sobs back that were crowding together in her chest and blocking her throat.

"Hey, hey." An awkward hand patted her shoulder. "Take your time."

She was glad he hadn't said it's fine, because nothing was fine. The pressure eased. She sucked in a deep breath, releasing it slowly in a shuddering sigh. Once she felt her control was in place again, she opened her eyes and stared into a set of deep brown eyes inches from her face. She blinked and leaned away.

Sergeant Beck moved back, discomfort stamped on his face. He apparently didn't feel up to comforting distraught women. It was an endearing quality.

"Sorry." She barely recognized the husky emotion-clogged voice coming from her mouth. "The note is still in the car. I'd given it to my mom..."

Except Linda Graham wasn't her mom, was she?

"You'd given it to your mom," Sergeant Beck encouraged.

She nodded. "Yes. She dropped it when she saw it. I picked it up. We packed our bags in record time. I'm pretty sure it's in our car, somewhere."

"In your mom's purse?"

She shook her head. "She didn't even know I'd picked it up. In the trunk or in one of my bags."

"We'll check your possessions. If it is not in

your bags, I'm sure the Crime Scene Unit has found it if it was in the car."

Joss held back a shudder. There was something truly awful about hearing the words "Crime Scene Unit" flowing so casually from his lips as they discussed the events of the day. She wanted to ask what he thought they would find but decided she didn't want to face the answers. She was feeling fragile enough now and wasn't sure how much more she could take.

"We should check your mom's stuff, too, just in case she saw it and took it back."

Not likely. She recalled the way her mom had dropped the note, as if it were a poisonous snake. Still, the cop was trying to cover all the bases. She'd let him do his job.

He left to go check her mom's belongings and she had nothing but her thoughts to keep her company. She slid down against the pillow and spent the next fifteen minutes struggling to not think of all that had occurred. To keep her mind occupied, she recited song lyrics in her head. It was a relief when the cop returned.

"Did you find anything?" Joss pushed herself back into a sitting position.

He shook his head. "Nope. I'm guessing you left it in the car. I'll check with evidence."

The curtain swung back. A different nurse

than the one who'd drawn her blood strode in. "I have your discharge papers and instructions from the doctor, honey. You might have some aches and pains from the accident. Take ibuprofen for them. No aspirin. If your headache returns, or if your vision changes or you feel dizzy or nauseous, come back immediately. Sign here."

She held the clipboard and pen to Joss and pointed to where she needed a signature.

"My mother?"

The woman shook her head. "I can't give you an update yet. Once you feel up to it, you can go back and wait in the waiting room."

In other words, they needed the bed she was occupying. "I'm good now."

Joss hopped down, and Sergeant Beck was there to steady her.

"I'll walk you to the waiting room before I leave." He ushered her ahead of him.

Before he left. Panic flared in her gut. She'd be left here, alone, not knowing the truth, with a killer looking for her. When he held the emergency door open, she found her voice.

"Wait. You're leaving me?" Her pitch climbed with each word.

He gave her a level stare, as if assessing how much he could tell her. "Miss Graham—"

"Joss," she reminded him. She didn't know if she really was a Graham at this point, and frankly, didn't want to think about the implications of that.

He ducked his head once. "Fine. Joss. You belong here until you hear about your mother. We'll have to run through the events of the day later. But first I need to see if I can locate that note."

They'd arrived at the waiting area. No one else was there. Even the receptionist was gone. It wouldn't last for long, however. She could hear a distant pager warning of three ambulances arriving. Sergeant Beck's radio came to life. He frowned as the dispatcher announced a multiple-car pileup and an interstate closure due to the weather.

"You can't leave me here by myself," she blurted. "I saw his face. The shooter. He looked right into my eyes. If you leave me by myself, he'll come for me."

She'd survived once. How long would she remain alive once the shooter realized she hadn't perished in the crash?

Haunted. There was no other way to describe the expression on Joss's face. Steve hovered near her elbow. He knew how it felt to have your entire life upended in the blink of an eye. Fifteen years ago, his entire family had been stolen from him when his alcoholic father had gotten behind the wheel of the family car and drifted into oncoming traffic. His mother and his ten-year-old twin sisters had never had a chance.

If he'd been with them, he might have been dead, too.

It might as well have been yesterday. There were some wounds that never completely healed.

He had to move and get this investigation going. But he also couldn't abandon a shooting victim. Even if she weren't the sole witness, she was a human being, and one who'd been through a harrowing day with no signs of getting better.

Holding back a sigh, he yanked his cell phone from his pocket. "I'll be right back."

Leaving the waiting area, he walked far enough away so he could talk privately while still keeping Joss in sight. He dialed evidence.

"Good afternoon. McCoy here."

Officer McCoy was a relatively new officer. He'd only met her a few times, but she was competent and efficient.

"Hey, Melissa. This is Steve Beck. Has the

CSU brought in the evidence from a car shooting this afternoon?" He kept his voice low in case it would echo in the open area with no carpeting to absorb sound.

"You have good timing," Melissa responded. He heard her moving items around on her end. "It was dropped off less than an hour ago."

"Perfect. I need you to check on something for me. There should have been a note logged in the evidence." He briefly described it, then waited while she checked the log, scuffing the toe of his left foot against the tile floor as he listened to the telltale noises of her search.

"Sorry, Steve. No such note here."

Steve lifted his eyes from the ground and frowned. Not there? That was odd. The CSU was very thorough. Where could it have gone? He shifted his gaze to Joss. She had stood and was moving around but didn't come over to where he was.

He disconnected and dialed his chief, watching Joss pacing in the waiting area while he waited for the phone to be picked up. The chief answered on the third ring.

"Chief Spencer. What do you have for me, Sergeant?"

"Chief, I'm still at the hospital. There's been a bit of a hiccup."

"Describe what you mean by 'hiccup.'"

Succinctly, Steve brought his commanding officer up to date.

The chief didn't respond immediately. He was a man who pondered all the facts before deciding how to react. Steve respected that. There was some clicking on the chief's end.

"Hold on for a second. I'm looking at Francesca's schedule on Outlook right now. She won't be available for four days. She's out of the county completely."

Francesca Brown was the forensic artist Sutter Springs Police Department used. Unfortunately, they were a small department and couldn't afford her full-time. She contracted with multiple precincts in Ohio and even part of Pennsylvania and was in high demand. Which meant sometimes they had to wait.

"What do you want me to do? I believe Miss Graham is in danger. She says she saw the shooter."

"I trust your instincts. I can't spare anyone right now. There's a mess on the interstate."

"I heard."

"I'm leaving you in charge of the witness for the time being, Sergeant. You good with that?" The chief's voice strongly suggested that it was a rhetorical question. Steve didn't actually have a choice. Not that he'd argue. His conscience would never allow him to abandon her while danger lurked.

"Yes, sir. I'll be heading over to the impound to check out the vehicle."

"That shouldn't be a problem. Hal and Princess are on duty." Amusement lurked in the chief's voice.

Steve laughed under his breath and hung up. Princess was a very large guard dog with a hair-raising growl, although she wasn't much more than a puppy. He couldn't imagine a dog who looked less like a *Princess*.

A harried receptionist returned to the front desk. Steve approached her. "Could you tell me the status of Linda Graham? I need to leave with her daughter for a bit if it's convenient."

She lifted a finger, asking him to wait for a moment, then picked up a phone to check. He leaned against the counter and waited. After a brief conversation, she disconnected. "The doctor has placed Miss Graham in the ICU. She's not woken up yet. Her condition is listed as serious."

It could still go either way. He hated that he couldn't ease Joss's mind.

Reaching into his coat pocket, he grabbed a stack of business cards and separated one from the rest. He handed the receptionist a card with his cell phone number on it. "Can you call this number if there are any changes?"

She wrote a short note on the card. "Yes, Officer."

Never one to put off the inevitable, he headed across the hall to the woman anxiously await-ing his return. When he approached her, Joss faced him, her shoulders squared. She expected him to leave her. Well, she'd have to learn that he took his responsibilities seriously.

"Your mother is in serious condition, but she's out of surgery."

Her chin dropped. She didn't say anything. He took a step closer.

"I called my chief. He said I could keep you with me." Her head popped up at that, eyes wide. "I gave the receptionist my number. She'll call me if there's any changes. I'd like to go to the impound before it's closed up for the night. Does that sound okay?"

She nodded slowly. "Yeah. Serious condition is better than critical."

She didn't sound like she thought it was much better. But then again, hadn't someone told him she worked in a doctor's office? She would know all the terminology and what it meant.

"I'd like to see her," she said.

He understood her desire, but he really wanted to check on the car before anyone else got to it.

"I doubt they're allowing visitors right now. I promise we'll get you into her room as soon as we can."

She frowned but nodded.

"Come on, let's go. Maybe we can be back in an hour or so." Steve glanced at the clock on the wall. They needed to move if he was going to search the car while it was still daylight. "I'll explain more of what's going on in the car."

It was still snowing outside, and the parking lot was coated with a light glaze of fluffy flakes. It was pretty, but also deceptively icy. Steve held onto her arm, keeping her close to his side. "Careful. Those boots aren't exactly made for walking distances in this weather."

Why did women wear heels in these conditions?

A soft snort answered him. "I know. But I'm short."

Huh. He hadn't really noticed, only being about five foot nine himself. Her head barely came to his shoulder. Taking off the two-inch heels, he'd place her at hovering around five foot nothing. Still, she'd need to find different shoes if they were together any length of time.

Later. They were on a deadline now, since he'd told her they'd try to be back in an hour.

After they reached his vehicle, he held the door of his cruiser open, then strode around to the driver's side. Activating the wipers and the window defrosters, he waited until his windshield and rear window cleared. Once he could see, he threw the cruiser into Reverse, placed his arm over the seat and twisted around to watch out the back window while he backed out of the narrow parking space.

"You have a backup camera," his passenger noted.

"Yeah. Don't trust those things." He left the parking lot and headed east. "So, here's the plan—I need you to sit with the forensic artist, but she's not available until Monday. The chief agreed to let me remain with you until we find the shooter."

The woman next to him readjusted her position. Her gaze scoured his profile. Steve's skin warmed under her intense perusal. When she turned her head away, he relaxed in his seat.

"What do you think it means, the note?"

He shrugged. "Your guess is probably the same as mine."

"But I want your opinion."

He hesitated, then plowed on. Hiding the

truth never solved any issues. Begin as you mean to continue, or so he'd heard. He never lied, and he wasn't about to start with Joss. "Frankly, I don't think we count out any scenarios. Whether it means she's not really Linda Graham or maybe she's hiding from something. The fact that there was a note and a sniper tells me whatever she's running from, it's big. And deadly."

She breathed out a wobbly sigh that just about ripped his heart apart. "I have no clue what she's running from. She's never said, and we'd been in one place for so long, I forgot to question. I can't trust anyone."

"You can trust me, Joss. I'm not going to leave you."

He pulled into the impound. Inside the fence, the twisted remains of her car taunted them. Turning the ignition off, he heard nothing except their breathing.

He said a silent prayer that his protection would be sufficient to keep the vibrant young woman sitting so close to him alive and safe from the unknown menace intent on murder.

THREE

Exiting the cruiser, Steve visually swept the horizon. The shadows were beginning to lengthen, but nothing jumped out at him. Still, he didn't let his guard down. His intuition was telling him something wasn't right. He couldn't leave Joss in the car. Reluctance made him pause. There was no way he'd bring a civilian into a dangerous situation. But what choice did he have? He either had to leave her alone in the car or bring her with him into the building.

Once they were inside, she'd be fine. It was the space between the car and the building that concerned him.

"Hey, Steve. What are you hanging out in the cold for?" Hal Johnson roared at him from the doorway, his face half-hidden behind his thick beard. His reddish-brown hair stood at various angles on his head.

Steve grinned and waved, his concerns melting away. Despite his somewhat fierce appearance, Hal was a gentle soul. He was also a huge man, standing at six foot four. Most people would hesitate before taking him on. He opened the passenger side door. "Come on, Joss."

She unbuckled her seat belt and stared past the open door, her eyes lighting on the Guard Dog on Premises sign, uncertainty dancing across her features. "Sergeant Beck—"

"Steve," he corrected her. If they were going to be stuck with each other for the next few days, formality would grow old fast. "Don't worry. I've known Hal for years. He's as steady as they come."

She didn't comment but kept close to his side as they made their way over to the building. The impound yard was connected to Hal's Autobody and Car Repair Shop. The mechanic led them to an office where a small space heater whirred in the corner. Hal didn't have a central system. It was too expensive to heat a building with huge doors that opened and closed on a regular basis, letting all the warmth escape.

Before sitting down, Steve glanced around the room. "Princess?"

"Relax, dude." Hal waved his concern away. "I have her in the next room. She won't come in until you're gone."

"Princess?" Joss asked, her brows elevated.

Hal chuckled. "Yeah. She's my new guard dog. I'm still training her, and she shows promise, but she's still too green to have her in here when strangers come to call."

Steve wiped his mouth with the back of his hand to hide his smile. Hal treated his dogs like they were his children. Joss glanced with trepidation to the door Hal had indicated, her shoulders tense.

Hmm. Was she cautious due to the dog's lack of training? Something in her posture told Steve it was more than that. He sensed that Joss Graham had a fear of dogs in general. He recalled her expression when she saw the sign. That would explain her hesitation in leaving the car.

"It's okay," he whispered to her. "Hal keeps that door locked. You won't see Princess while we're here. And I understand—I have a phobia of snakes myself."

Color rose in her cheeks, but her shoulders relaxed.

Hal smiled at her. "I'll keep her locked up. You don't need to worry."

Steve cleared his throat and Hal glanced at him. "I want to go look at a car brought in this afternoon. It was the one in the shooting."

Hal tilted his head. "Only car that's arrived today. Why? It's been processed."

"Yeah, but I think they missed something."

Hal's bushy eyebrows disappeared under his hair.

"Seriously? That's hard to believe." Hal stood and grabbed a key from the hook. "I can let you inside the fence."

"Can you wait here?" Steve turned to Joss. "I don't want you standing out in the open. If you're in here, Hal can look after you."

"And Princess is a good deterrent, even locked in the other room," Hal interjected, shoving his arms into a thick winter coat. "I'll be right back."

"I can let myself in," Steve objected.

"One minute, Steve. Then I'll be back. You know nothing is going to happen to the girl in that time. Not without either you or me noticing. Anyway, I'll lock her in. And if someone tries to get in the other door, Princess will take care of them."

It was true. And Hal never let anyone take hold of his keys. Not even the cops. Steve agreed but wasn't happy about it. Something about not being in control of all the details made him edgy.

Joss rose from her seat. Her teeth worried her

full bottom lip, and her face was pale, but she didn't complain or argue. Nor did she attempt to delay him. He admired her grit.

"Where do you think the note would be?"

She lifted her hands. "I'm not sure. I had it with me while I packed my bags. I'm pretty certain it's in the bag with my Bible and other books. It's a canvas bag that doesn't seal up. They were all in the trunk. I'm thinking the note might have fallen out when the bags shifted during the crash."

"Right. So, I'll start in the trunk and move forward. Just in case it wasn't in the trunk."

"Steve," she said, frowning. "We went into the house when she—my mom—insisted we pack our bags. What if I'm wrong and I didn't grab it off my bed? What if the note's there, instead?"

He nodded. "In all seriousness, that seems a lot more likely than the CSU missing it. They're very thorough. However, we're here. I might as well check so we don't have to backtrack again. If I don't find the note here, we'll search the house, too." He left his place near the door to approach her and set a hand on her shoulder. "Joss, I'd want to search there, as well, no matter what we find here. I'm interested in any clues that will lead to the arrest of the man who shot at you."

He held her eyes for a few seconds before letting his hand drop and motioning to Hal. The mechanic smiled at Joss before leading the way outside. Following Hal to the fence, he kept glancing behind, checking for anything suspicious. When he looked at the building he'd recently left, Joss's face watching him through the window eased his agitation.

She was fine. He hadn't failed her. She was still alive and well.

He'd keep her that way, too. He waved her away from the window. She was too easy a target there. She nodded and disappeared. Even though he knew she was safer, no longer having her in sight had adrenaline spiking in his system. He needed to do this—fast.

Once Hal unlocked the gate, Steve watched him until he had disappeared back into the office. Not until then did he relax his vigilance. He needed to check through the car. He started in the trunk, lifting floor mats and probing into all the nooks and crannies. Any little crevice was a possible hiding place for the note that had started Joss and Linda's flight.

At least one bullet had pierced the trunk. The Crime Scene Unit had collected any casings left behind. Not even a shred of evidence remained.

He moved on to the back seat. Again, there

was nothing of significance left behind. The glass from the shattered back window had been removed. Not a single shard remained. The surety that he was on a wild goose chase strengthened. He knew it was improbable he'd find anything in the car, but he had to check. Hopefully, when they searched the house, he'd find some answers there.

Once he was convinced he'd searched every spot in the back seat, he moved to the front. Opening the door, his flashlight caught a dark stain on the floorboard. Was it a stain from something spilled in the past? Or was it blood?

Acid churned in his stomach. He knew it was Linda's blood. Had she lost consciousness before the car had hit the guardrail? And what about Joss? He eyed the dashboard. Where had her head hit it? The bruise on her forehead was so large he was amazed she didn't have a concussion. He eyed the stain again. She must have been terrified. Steve wrenched his mind away from stain. A light flashed in the mirror. Straightening to stand outside the vehicle, he surveyed the area. He couldn't see or hear anything wrong, but his gut told him he needed to hurry.

Steve was inclined to listen to his intuition. He needed to complete his job here and return to Joss. Once he'd finished, he'd hurry her out of Hal's office as fast as he could without risking her injuring herself in a fall. Only then would the knot in his shoulders disappear.

Joss rubbed her arms briskly, shivering. Even with her coat on, she was frozen clear down to her bones. She wasn't sure she'd ever be warm again. Despite the heater, the room was still chilly. A few degrees colder and she'd be able to see her breath. She rubbed her hands in front of her mouth and puffed, trying to warm them with her breath.

At least Hal was back.

When he and Steve had left earlier, she had watched out the window until Steve had waved her back. When she realized someone could shoot her through it, she'd stood against the wall beside the filing cabinet until Hal had rejoined her. The large man had entered, patted her on the shoulder and sank down into a chair behind his desk. It creaked and groaned. He ignored it.

She watched him plunking away on his keyboard, his bushy brows drawn together in concentration. She contemplated him, smiling. He tapped on the keyboard with his index fingers, one letter at a time.

Yawning, he sat tall and caught her grin. She flushed, but Hal laughed. "I bet you're wondering why I didn't take keyboarding or typing classes in high school." He waggled his digits at her. "I did, but my fingers are too large to type without errors. My teachers gave up on me."

"That's terrible!"

He shrugged. "Nah. I get along just fine. I hope you don't mind, miss, but I have to complete this invoice. I don't mean to be rude."

She gestured for him to proceed, relieved she wouldn't be expected to converse. She didn't want to be rude either, but she would have trouble holding up her end of any conversation. Her mind was mush. Grief ate at her. She couldn't shake the image of her poor mother wedged against the side of the car bleeding. What if she never woke up? Joss pulled her sweater away from her neck, attempting to ease the tightness in her throat. Even if Linda had lied to Joss, she refused to believe the loving mother who had raised her alone had ever done anything that would cause this sort of retribution. Would she ever again have the opportunity to tell her mom she loved her? That she forgave her for whatever mistakes she'd made?

A grinding noise roused her from her dark musings. It took a second to recognize the sound of a printer starting up in the next room. Relieved, she sagged against the wall, her face heating with embarrassment. She wasn't usually this skittish.

Hal stood and stretched, letting out another enormous yawn. "Well, that finishes that one. I'm going to get that invoice and a fresh cup of coffee."

Her eyes flashed to the door behind his desk, her stomach twisting. She did not want to come face-to-face with a dog.

"Relax. I can go through the garage to get to the printer. Princess is in a different room."

She wilted back against the wall. Hal sauntered away from his desk, stopping when he was a foot from her, his hand on the doorknob to the garage bay.

"You want anything? I can get you a cup of coffee, or I have Pepsi and water, too."

Until he mentioned it, Joss hadn't realized how thirsty she was. Suddenly, her throat was as dry as a desert. "A Pepsi would be great, thanks!"

"Sure thing." He gave her a thumbs-up and grinned before opening the door and disappearing behind it, whistling off-key. She smiled and shook her head.

Joss returned to the main door, standing to

the side and peering carefully around the edge of the window to watch Steve as he slowly and methodically searched the front seat. How long could it possibly take? It was a small car.

She was unaware of how much time had passed when she noticed the absolute silence around her. The hair on the back of her neck stood up. Something wasn't right. Avoiding the door Princess was behind, she edged closer to the one leading to the printer, opened it and peered out, skimming her glance through the dim garage bays. Hal was nowhere in sight. He'd left to get a cup of coffee and her Pepsi. It shouldn't have taken this long. Something had happened to him. Unsure of what to do, she stepped into the garage, shivering at the sudden drop in temperature. The door swung closed behind her.

"Hal?" she whispered.

No response. She needed to get Steve.

Turning back to the door, she fumbled with the knob. It was locked. Her blood froze in her veins. She had stranded herself in the garage with no way to contact Steve. Her heartbeat ratcheted up. Blood pounded in her ears, drowning out any other sounds.

Think, Joss.

Maybe she could find another door leading

outside. If she could find a way out, she could get to Steve. He'd be able to handle whatever had happened to Hal. Fear closed her throat. She needed to pray but was unable to form a coherent thought. *Please, Lord. Please.*

Keeping close to the walls, she made her way around the garage, stopping every few feet to listen. She forced herself to breathe slowly and quietly. The light in the garage dimmed further each minute. January in Ohio meant the sun set by five thirty each evening. As the room darkened, the chill in it deepened.

What was taking Steve so long? And why couldn't she find another door?

Finally, after following another wall, she located a door. The breath whooshed from her in a quiet sigh. Even if it opened to the area at the back of the garage, she could slip around to the front easily enough. Behind her, she heard a racket as Princess began to bark in earnest. She shuddered. That was one dog she never wanted to come face-to-face with. It sounded like the animal was crashing against the door, trying to get into the main part of the garage. What if the dog broke through? She needed to get into the room and find Hal now.

Reaching for the knob, her hand shook. She grimaced. Turning it, she was relieved to find it was unlocked. She pulled it open and slid through it, only to find it led to another room.

A hum in the corner of the room brought her up short.

She was in the room with the refrigerator. A microwave sat on the counter, its display blinking. The dim light coming through the windows allowed her to see a large figure spread out on the floor.

"Hal!"

He didn't move. Maybe he had a heart attack. She felt along the wall until her fingers bumped into a light switch. Flipping it, she blinked as light from the ceiling fixtures flooded the room. Her gaze fell on Hal.

A pool of blood surrounded him, his eyes open and staring blankly at her. A coffee mug lay shattered behind him and a dented Pepsi can was near his feet.

He was dead, and not from a heart attack. He'd been shot. How had someone discharged a gun without alerting her to their presence? Joss whimpered before she could stop herself. Someone had ambushed him while he was in here. Murdered a man who just wanted to get a cup of coffee.

She knew that Hal wasn't the intended victim. The shooter had come for her. A new thought struck, sending terror coursing through her veins. What if he had gotten to Steve, as well?

She had to get help. Steve had wanted her to remain indoors, but that was no longer a safe option.

Joss bounded through the open door and stopped. A large dog faced her, growling, its hackles raised.

Princess.

The dog's muscles quivered. It was getting ready to attack.

Whirling, she jumped into the room and slammed the door closed behind her two seconds before eighty pounds of angry dog pounced. The dog pounded against the closed door. The frame shook with the force of the blow. She was trapped. The door wouldn't last long. The building was old. With every hit, the hinges threatened to give way.

Joss sank down against the wall. She avoided glancing toward Hal, but her hope had run out. The only question in her mind was whether she'd be killed by a bullet or by the hound intent on breaking through the door.

FOUR

Steve slid his right knee off the seat and backed out of the car. Standing, he bumped the door closed with his hip while he peeled the latex gloves off his hands, then stuffed them in his pocket. As expected, he didn't find anything worth noting in the car. It was hard not to feel frustrated at the total waste of time, but it needed to be ruled out. At least now they could turn their attention to searching the house.

The sky was growing dim. Within twenty minutes, it would be too dark outside to see beyond his hand without a flashlight. Steve strode toward the office, the sound of snow crunching beneath his boots overly loud in the still twilight air. His breath puffed in front of his face as he breathed out. Nearing the building, he briskly rubbed his hands together to maintain warmth, then reached out to open the office door. His hand gripped the icy knob and he winced. He turned it.

Nothing happened.

The office was still locked. He knocked.

"Hal! It's me, Steve. Open up." When there was no response, he knocked and called again, louder this time.

Steve frowned. Normally, Hal would yell to hold on, but there was no response. Urgency coursed through his blood. Alternately yanking on the knob and pushing on the door, he attempted to force his way in. "Hal! Joss!"

Somewhere in the back of the building, a dog barked, a deep menacing sound. Princess. He listened to her for a few seconds, the hair on the back of his neck standing on end. This was different from the sounds she made earlier when they were in the office. This wasn't the barking of a puppy wanting out of the room. No, this was an enraged dog defending her territory.

Steve released the door now and ran around to the back of the building, his boots slipping on the slush and snow. He needed to get in there and see what was happening. Every instinct screamed Joss and Hal were in danger. If he couldn't enter through the office, he'd try to get in via the garage bay. There was a pedestrian door. Hal usually kept it locked to encourage customers and guests to enter through the office since he let Princess roam the bays when he was working. He didn't like customers coming in while she was free. Well, Steve would reimburse him for the cost of a broken door if necessary, but he was coming in, no matter what it took.

Rounding the corner of the building, Steve blinked against the glare of the setting sun breaking through the tree line. He threw up one hand to block the rays and stumbled to a halt in front of the door.

It was open partially, the window smashed.

His blood froze in his veins. Someone had gotten there before him. Someone had forced their way in despite a cop in the parking lot and a guard dog on the premises. He was dealing with a desperate individual. The question was were they still inside?

Releasing his Glock from his holster, he slid the weapon free and held it before him, pointed down, then crept into the garage. Princess was in the main bay of the garage, standing on her hind legs, her front paws scratching and digging at the door to the break room. As he watched, she backed down and jumped at the door again, attempting to get at whatever was in the room. The old door shuddered in response to her weight.

How had she escaped from the room where Hal had kept her? Shifting his glance, he saw the splintered wood. That answered his question. The dog had broken through the door. But what would have caused her to do so?

Slowly, he approached her, keeping his hands out in front of him. Princess knew him. She'd let him pet her. Hopefully, it would be enough to keep her from attacking him.

"Princess." He pitched his voice low.

She stopped attacking the door and ran to him, whining frantically, before running back to the door. Her paws stamped on the ground.

He had to get into that room. What was in there? If he recalled, it was the break room. Hal and his part-time assistant would eat meals in there when they had time for lunch.

"Easy, girl. I'm going to open the door."

"Steve?"

He froze.

"Joss? Are you okay?"

She sobbed behind the door. "Hal's hurt. I think he's dead. And the dog…"

Now he understood. "I'm coming to get you, Joss. Keep away from the door, okay? And get as far away from Hal as you can."

Behind the door, he heard her scurrying to do what he'd asked. When the noise had ceased, he approached Princess.

"Princess, sit."

The dog whined, but her hindquarters lowered to the garage floor. She quivered, ready to move. The poor thing was desperate to get to Hal. He hurried to the coat hooks on the wall and grabbed the leash there. Hal took Princess on a walk along the property lines every morning. Steve hooked the leash to the loop on her collar. Princess whined at him. A lump clogged his throat.

"Okay, Princess. Let's go to Hal."

Holding her leash tight, Steve pushed the door open. Princess strained forward. He led her into the room.

Princess ignored Joss and went straight to Hal's prone body. Whining, she laid her head on his chest.

Steve stepped close to his friend and knelt on one knee beside him. Hal's eyes were trained on the ceiling. Steve knew he was dead before he reached out to verify the fact. He could see the gunshot wound. The perp must have used a silencer. Otherwise, he or Joss would have heard the attack. He bowed his head, sadness overwhelming him. He'd brought this danger to his friend.

"Steve?" Joss whispered.

He lifted his head to see the woman who was inadvertently the reason for Hal's demise. Her large brown eyes met his, sorrow and pain etched on her face. "I'm sorry. I should have stayed at the hospital."

Princess whined. Joss's head jerked.

"She won't hurt you." He stood with a sigh, pulling his phone out to call 911 and notify the chief. "None of this is your fault, Joss. Whether or not the person who did this was searching for you doesn't matter. You didn't do anything to make this happen. You are as much a victim as he is."

He kept his eyes on her as he made the call. She didn't appear to believe him, but dispatch answered before he had a chance to try to reassure her again. "Leslie, Sergeant Beck here. I need backup at Hal's Auto. There's been a shooting. Hal is down."

The dispatcher gasped in his ear. Everyone knew and loved the large mechanic.

Steve fought to keep his emotions under control and continued. "I need the coroner and EMS to stage nearby until the scene has been searched."

Once dispatch had been taken care of, he called the chief. He clenched his teeth to hold his emotions at bay as he updated Chief Spencer.

"Steve, did you see the shooter?"

"No, sir. I think Princess broke out of her room and chased him off before I got back in the building." He shut his eyes. "If I'd been quicker—"

"Sergeant Beck." Chief's stern voice broke through his remorse. "You did your job. Keep your head in the game. We have to catch this guy. I need you at your best."

"I understand, sir." He didn't have the luxury to wallow in the endless abyss of what-ifs. Anyway, it would be a waste of his time, not to mention the drain it would have on his mental energy. Joss needed him to be one hundred percent focused on the case. Bottling up the emotions roiling in his gut, he set about doing his job.

He needed to find this man, this killer who had gone after Joss and her mother and had murdered a good man.

Joss backed against the wall, pressing herself into it and pulling her legs up to her chest. She wrapped her arms around them, tight. If she could have disappeared into the faux wood-work, she would have. The terror she'd felt when she'd first glimpsed Princess had dropped several notches since Steve had entered the room. It was strange, but he made her feel safe, despite the evidence that a killer was on the loose. Still, she shuddered every time the dog whined.

Was Hal's death somehow related to the shooting that had put her mother in the hospital? She squeezed her lids closed as the image of a man with cold eyes aiming a gun at her invaded her mind. She wasn't sure how it all tied together, but deep inside, she knew the two horrendous situations were linked.

But how?

Steve sighed. She winced. It was her fault his friend was dead, her fault he was feeling such guilt and loss. If she hadn't insisted on coming with him, maybe the killer wouldn't have come this way. She burrowed her head into her arms. Her body shook.

"Joss, are you okay?"

Her head jerked up. She hadn't noticed Steve approaching her. Heat flared in her cheeks. How long had he been watching her? The moment the thought flashed through her brain, she straightened, firming her lips. She'd never been one to let something so trivial get to her.

Deep lines framed his mouth. Those hadn't been there earlier. Grief over Hal's death had carved them. A part of her shattered inside. She'd caused this.

"I'm sorry," she blurted. "I never meant for any of this to happen. For Hal to get killed, or for anyone to get hurt because of me."

He crouched in front of her, cutting off her words. Those deep brown eyes stared into hers. "Don't."

"You know it's the same guy. You know this isn't a coincidence."

He dipped his head, acknowledging her point. "Yeah, probably."

She snorted. "Definitely."

"Still. Joss, this isn't your fault. This person, whoever he is, has no qualms hurting innocent people. He would have attacked you, and anyone near you, no matter where you were. I'm convinced of it."

Wow. Her stomach bottomed out. Nowhere was safe. If she went back to the hospital, would her presence endanger the people there? Or was the hospital safe because of the sheer number of witnesses?

The wind kicked up outside, the howling echoing her internal chaos. She wrapped her arms around her middle to hold it all in.

"Where can I go, Steve? I don't want anyone else to get hurt because someone is hunting me."

Tension flickered across his face, tightened his eyes.

"You aren't going anywhere alone. You are staying with me. I will do everything in my power to keep you safe and find who hurt your mother. But you're going to need to trust me and do what I say. Can you do that?"

Following orders might cause some internal strife. She'd never liked being told what to do, but she wouldn't argue. "I won't do anything dumb. I know you have more experience in these matters."

He nodded and stood, moving away from her and back over to where Hal lay. Her heart ached. Princess lifted her head to watch Steve. Joss had never known an animal could look sad. She'd never had any pets growing up, no doubt because her mother knew they might flee in a hurry and wouldn't be able to take pets with them. What would happen to the dog now?

She heard the sirens thirty seconds before the lights flashed through the window.

"Backup's here," Steve announced, his voice quiet.

Two minutes later, they were joined by

three other police officers. She didn't catch their names first, but the female officer's uniform had the lieutenant insignia, although she couldn't read her name from where she sat. The unknown lieutenant took charge and directed the others to search the building and the perimeter.

"Someone needs to stay with Miss Graham, Kathy," Steve stated. "This is the second attack in several hours. If the perp is still around, he might make another attempt on her life."

He turned to Joss. "This is Lieutenant Bartlett." Then he pointed to the other two officers. "And these are Officers Hansen and Zilhaver."

Lieutenant Bartlett nodded to Joss before responding to his earlier comments. "You have a valid point, Steve. Someone should stand guard here. Would you remain with our witness?"

He clasped his hands behind his back and nodded.

Guilt pierced her again. Now he had to play babysitter rather than going out and doing his job.

He flicked a narrow glare her way. "Don't think it. It's fine."

How did he know what she was thinking?

She bit back a retort and watched the other

police officers depart. Within minutes, the sounds of the garage and the outside yard being searched filtered into the break room. Steve's radio crackled. Lieutenant Bartlett's voice echoed from several radios. "The scene is safe. Send in the coroner and the EMS crew."

The dispatcher's voice replaced that of the lieutenant. Multiple pagers, carried by the officers in the building, came to life with a burst of static. The waiting teams began to call in. Princess lifted her head with a chilling growl at the noise.

Joss cringed. None of the others seemed worried. Lieutenant Bartlett bent down to rub the dog's ears. "Easy, girl. It's all right."

The dog closed her eyes and settled down, heaving a weary sigh.

Inside the break room, Joss felt like she'd been transported onto the set of a crime scene television program. Law enforcement and Crime Scene Unit investigators swarmed the small area. Joss tried to be invisible, hunched against the wall, while keeping an eye on Princess.

"You don't have to be afraid of her." Steve squatted at her side, his forearms resting casually on his knees. "I know she's big and she's got a mean growl, but Princess has been trained well enough to not chase anyone who doesn't make threatening moves. Plus, you're with me, and she knows I'm a friend."

Joss squirmed under his scrutiny, feeling like a bug under a microscope. Willing him to back up and give her some breathing room, she dropped her eyes to the floor. When he didn't move, she sighed and gave in.

"I know it probably sounds ridiculous to you, but I'm just not comfortable with dogs."

"Were you attacked?"

She grimaced at the sympathy twined through the words.

"No, nothing like that." She finally met his level stare. "I've never had a pet. Not even a goldfish. My mom said they would be too hard to take care of. But now I'm wondering if it was because she was scared we'd have to pick up and move again. She'd never abandon any creature, so traveling with a pet would have been a hardship. I think she might have worried a pet would slow us down if we needed to leave fast in a hurry."

"Hmm." He nodded slowly. "Yeah, I can see that. And you'd get attached to a pet."

"True." Her mother would have hated tearing her away from a pet she'd grown to love. "What will happen to Princess?"

Steve pushed himself to his feet. "She'll be fine. The department can always use another K-9. She's young, so we should be able to get her properly trained."

Officer Zilhaver entered the room, a man muffled in a fur-trimmed coat on his heels. The newcomer slipped his hands into latex gloves as he walked. He had a face made for sitting around a campfire and telling stories. Instead, his features radiated with purpose. He passed her and raised his eyebrows. Joss offered a grimace in return. She'd known Dane Lenz for years. No one worked in a hospital or doctor's office in Sutter Springs without occasionally running into the county coroner.

Apparently, Dane was known to Princess. The large dog moved away from Hal with a high-pitched sound that reminded Joss of a nail dragging across a metal surface. The coroner barely even reacted. He went about his business efficiently. So calmly, in fact, that it would have been easy to take his professional demeanor as cold or uncaring. But Joss knew better.

In a remarkably short time, Dane declared Hal's death murder, citing a gunshot wound as the cause of death. The mechanic was placed in a body bag and Officer Zilhaver and Steve lifted it onto a stretcher as if he were made of

porcelain. She gathered herself off the floor and
trailed after the somber group, who watched
Hal's body be transferred to Dane's van. A single security light in the middle of the parking
lot had come on, illuminating the area enough
to see the expressions on those around her.
No one said anything during the process. In
a matter of minutes, the four cops gathered in
a solemn line for a silent send-off. Joss swallowed, touched by the sign of respect for Hal.
She gently wedged herself between Steve and
Lieutenant Bartlett. Both officers shifted their
stance to make room for Joss without remov-
ing their attention from the coroner's van as it
moved beyond the crime scene tape marking
the perimeter.

"I'll take Princess with me." Lieutenant
Bartlett's voice disturbed the silence. "I'll also
stop by the station and begin the paperwork and
update the chief. We need to work efficiently
to catch this guy."

Steve nodded once. "I'll remain behind to
turn the scene over to the CSU."

"Sure. Sounds like a plan. I can take the witness back with me, too, and drop her off at the
hospital."

The witness? Wait. That was her. Joss edged
herself so close to Steve, she was practically

snuggled against his side. No way. She wasn't going with a stranger. Especially not a stranger who would have a very large German shepherd in her police car.

Not only that, but she'd be taking up the lieutenant's time when she could be working to find Hal's killer. Did she really have time to stop by the hospital?

A hand squeezed her elbow. Startled, she flicked her eyes up at Steve. He lifted one shoulder in a shrug. "Joss? Kathy would bring you back to the hospital. I might be here for a while. I'll stop by later."

"I'd rather stay with you." The desire to be with her mother warred with the knowledge that she'd be taking Kathy out of her way, and every second counted in the search for a killer.

Kathy Bartlett grunted. "Fine. Stay. I think you should keep the dog with you, then."

That wasn't exactly what Joss wanted to hear. Steve opened his mouth, possibly to argue, then seemed to change his mind. "Do that."

Kathy turned on her heel and stalked off to her cruiser. Doors slammed as Officers Hansen and Zilhaver followed suit. Princess settled in beside Joss, her tongue lolling out of her mouth. She seemed friendly enough now, but Joss inched away from her.

"Steve," Joss hissed. "Why didn't you tell her to take Princess? You know we'll be stuffed into the same car when the CSU gets here."

"I know." He faced her. "Joss, I know you're scared of big dogs. I also know there's a killer out there. If you are insisting on staying with me, I think that Princess will be helpful in protecting you. Hopefully, I'm overthinking things. But I've learned that it's better to be overprepared."

Her lips tightened around the argument that threatened to escape from her mouth. Ducking her head, she watched her toe kicking at the snow on the ground. He didn't have to keep her with him, she reminded herself. In fact, his job would be a whole lot easier without her tagging along. Regardless of whether she liked it or not, she would have to deal with the dog's presence. Princess stretched her mouth open in a yawn. Joss couldn't help but notice how sharp her teeth were. Seeing them, her stomach quivered.

Lights spilled into the darkness, the beam moving in a wide arc as a vehicle pulled deeper into the parking lot. Automatically, her muscles tautened. Princess leaned her bulk against Joss's leg. No doubt the pooch was trying to comfort Joss, unaware of her fears.

"Here comes the CSU now." Steve headed toward the car.

The tension leaked from her shoulders. She followed him. Soon, they could go back to the hospital. Reluctant to interfere with his work, she halted before she reached where Steve stood talking with the members of the Crime Scene Unit. Princess padded to her side, her paws making a bare whisper of sound on the snow-covered ground.

After a couple of minutes, Steve separated from the newcomers and motioned Joss over. She rolled her eyes but began to move in his direction. Suddenly, Princess was there, blocking her path, lips pulled back in a vicious snarl. The dog growled, staring off to the left.

She knew what it meant.

Someone was out there.

FIVE

Steve whirled toward Joss. "Down!"

Her eyes widened a moment before Princess charged past him and jumped on her, barreling her to the ground, muffling Joss's resulting shriek with her fur. A bullet whizzed through the space Joss had been standing in half a second earlier. It smashed into the frozen parking lot with a puff of snow.

"I didn't hear a shot!" Joss gasped.

"Go inside!" Steve waited until she'd scrambled to her feet and disappeared inside the building before taking off in the direction of the shot. He knew the CSU members were inside gathering evidence and taking pictures.

He'd thought the scene was safe. Otherwise, he'd never have allowed her to be out in the open and vulnerable. Kathy and her team had crawled over the area, too. Which meant whoever was taking shots at Joss had come back.

For her.

If he'd harbored any doubts about who the real target was, they would have vanished the instant that bullet tried to take Joss out.

Princess howled and bounded out in front of him. He leaned forward and pressed himself to run harder. He'd let the dog lead him to the sniper. She darted behind an old, dilapidated shed, its paint peeling and the entire structure leaning to one side. Steve swerved around the small building in time to see the German shepherd's heavy tail vanish into the trees. Forging ahead, he pounded after her.

For a moment, he couldn't see anything. Grabbing the small flashlight he kept in his interior coat pocket, he flipped it on and kept moving forward, his pace slower now that Princess was out of his line of sight. Not to mention the plethora of branches and tripping hazards littering the ground. He would be no use to Joss or the investigation with a broken leg.

Ahead of him, Princess growled. A surprised yell transformed into a scream. Steve smiled with grim satisfaction. Princess had caught their perp. Picking up the pace, he followed the sounds of a dog growling and the man swearing and complaining in pain.

Rounding a massive tree, he slowed. Princess stood over a man, her snout inches from her prey, teeth glinting in the glare of the flashlight. On the ground, the man cowered, one arm blocking his face. His dark coat was ripped. It was hard to tell, but Steve was pretty sure he was bleeding from where the dog had caught him.

Most importantly, his gun lay two feet behind him. Princess had done her job well.

"Nice work, Princess. Stand down."

The dog's growl ceased. She sat back on her haunches, panting as if they'd been playing a simple game of fetch.

Steve kept his weapon trained on the man. "On your feet."

"Your dog bit me!" he blustered. "I could sue. You'll lose your job."

"I said. On. Your. Feet." Steve bit off each word, his anger growing every second. This man had tried to kill Joss. He'd put her mother in the hospital, fighting for her life. Steve pondered. How was he going to handcuff the perp? He couldn't risk putting down the flashlight, and he needed his gun.

Wait. He had Princess. He watched the man struggle to his feet, cradling his injured arm. "Don't move. Princess, guard."

The sniper flinched as Princess stood and approached him again. His gaze flicked to his gun.

"I wouldn't. She'll have you down before you can touch it."

Steve paused to be sure the man heeded his warning. Satisfied, he placed his flashlight on the ground, using the snow to plant it at an angle, forming an awkward spotlight on the sniper. Then Steve reached into his pocket and snagged his handcuffs.

"You are under arrest," he began, enunciating each word, "for the murder of Hal Johnson, the attempted murder of Joss Graham and the attempted murder of Linda Graham—"

"I never tried to kill anyone—"

Steve raised his voice above the protests. Grabbing one arm, then the other, he handcuffed the man's wrists behind his back. Ignoring the steady stream of invectives, he continued to read him his Miranda rights. "You have the right to remain silent…"

Hooking his right arm in a steely grip, Steve half marched, half dragged his captive back through the trees, retracing his steps to where he'd left Joss. He'd need to call another cruiser to come and get this guy. That would have to wait until he reached his vehicle. The sniper tugged, trying to pull his arm free. There was no way Steve was going to let that happen. Every time the man pulled, Steve tightened his hold. Finally, they arrived back at the car.

Opening the back door, Steve stuffed the shooter into the seat, placing a hand on his head so he wouldn't hit the top of the door frame as he lowered himself into the vehicle. Trying to sit when one's hands were cuffed was challenging.

Steve shut the door and locked it so he couldn't escape, then he contacted dispatch. A familiar voice responded.

"Hey, Leslie. I need another vehicle at Hal's."

"I'm on it, Beck."

He winced. Leslie's normally vibrant voice sounded muffled, as if she had a bad cold. Or had been crying. News of Hal's murder would hit them all hard. As much as he wanted to be comforting, he had a job to do and a woman to protect. "Listen, Leslie. Can you do me a solid? I want to let the CSU know there's an abandoned gun in the wooded area behind the shed. But I don't want to leave the perp unguarded."

"I'll do that right now."

He disconnected the call and waited. The seconds ticked by. A long minute later, one of the CSU team members trotted out.

"Where did you leave the gun?"

Steve gave him the approximate location. "You can probably follow our tracks. This guy was dragging his feet so much on the way back it might look like a whole Boy Scout troop marched through there."

Zach, the CSU investigator, snickered. "Nah. They'd be more careful to leave no trace."

Steve grinned at the familiar motto. Zach had been an Eagle Scout and was very proud of it.

A few minutes later, Officer Zilhaver swung back into the lot. "I wasn't far away when the call came in. Had to issue a traffic violation."

"Glad you were close. This guy tried to shoot at Joss Graham while we were in the parking lot. He's been read his rights. Take care of him for me?"

"Sure thing." It took only a minute to transfer the sniper from one car to another. "Where are you heading?"

"I need to get her back to the hospital. I want her to see her mom for a few minutes before visiting hours are done." He thought about that for a moment. "You know what, can you take Princess for me? Now that we've got our guy?"

"Gotcha." Zilhaver opened his front door and whistled. "Come on, Princess. In."

The canine loped over and jumped into the

passenger seat, sitting still and facing forward. Steve chuckled. She was a good dog.

The door to the garage slammed. Joss rushed over to where Steve was. He narrowed his gaze, zeroing in on her pale face. "Don't glare at me. I saw you move someone, so I assume you got him."

"Yeah." Steve shifted over to give her a clear view of the window. Zilhaver got behind the wheel and buckled up.

Some of his exhilaration died at her next words. "That's not the same man."

"Excuse me?" He frowned, confused. "This is the guy who shot at you. Princess brought him down."

She shook her head. "That's not what I meant. This is not the guy who shot my mom."

Zilhaver pulled away.

Steve ping-ponged his eyes between her and the man in the back of the police cruiser driving away from them.

Her words hit him like a linebacker. For a moment, he was too stunned to speak.

"Get in my car. It's not safe for you to stand out here."

She didn't hesitate to hop in the front seat. He joined her and sat behind the wheel. "I need a minute."

He ran a hand through his hair as he considered his options. "Okay. I need to call my chief and inform him of all this. We're going to go see your mom. Then you're not leaving my side until I am convinced you're safe. Not while we have no idea who is coming after you."

"I still can't figure out what the note meant."

Yeah, he'd wondered that, too.

"Joss, I'm not going to lie. This is all somehow connected with your mom. I won't rule out that she might have gotten herself in over her head in something."

He hated sounding negative, especially when she'd been through so much today, but he wouldn't lie to her. The impulse to reach over and pat her shoulder, offer some kind of comfort, took him by surprise. He wouldn't give in. He needed to keep his attention on the goal. If he didn't, he might miss something important. He wouldn't fail her the way he did his mom and sisters.

"I need to call the chief." Steve punched the call button on the dash. He listened to the phone ring, tapping his fingers on the steering wheel. The chief picked up on the third ring.

"Sergeant Beck. What do you have for me?" The chief's voice was heavy with sorrow. Yeah, he felt that way, too. Hal had been a good guy.

"Chief, Joss says the man at the auto garage was not the same man who shot at her and Linda Graham earlier today."

He and the chief talked through the possibilities. Then a new thought occurred to him. "I was wondering if we'd consider keeping Princess?"

"It's a possibility. I have Hal's brother coming in to identify the body and make arrangements. It will all depend on what he wants to do with her. If he has no use for her, the department will buy her from him."

They talked a few more minutes. Steve glanced over at Joss. She was pale and quiet. Too quiet. She was too young to have the weight of all this on her slim shoulders.

Not my problem. Except he couldn't shake the feeling if he didn't solve this case soon, Joss Graham would become a huge problem in his life.

Steve's words bounced around in her head the entire ride to the hospital. She shut out most of his conversation with his chief—she knew the salient information. In her gut, she trusted Steve to share whatever facts or plans she needed to know. It was enough for now. It was difficult to process everything that had happened in the past few hours. How much more could she take?

"We're not going to go to the house tonight." Steve's voice broke into her reverie.

"Oh?" She hadn't thought that far ahead.

"The chief wants you to get some rest, if you can. Then he wants you to go over the database and see if you can find the man who shot your mom. After that, we'll venture to the house. Hopefully, we'll find what we need there to shed some light on what's going on."

"I don't think I'll sleep peacefully again. Every time I close my eyes, I'll see that face—that man—pointing a gun at us. And my mother." A strangled sob worked its way up her throat and broke free. She slammed her mouth closed and squeezed her eyes shut, desperate to hold the tears at bay. She hated to cry in front of anyone. Steve's hand covered hers.

"I'm here to help you through this, Joss. We'll find him. Whoever is responsible. I'll get him."

She shook her head.

"You can't promise that." She grimaced. Her voice came out in a croak.

"I can promise to do everything in my power."

She turned her head to stare through the thick darkness blanketing the road. Every now and then, they'd pass a house with a light on the porch or shining through the window. It felt oppressive. When they emerged into the downtown area of Sutter Springs, small as it was, she breathed easier. The streetlamps lining the business district calmed her anxiety. For the past decade, she'd lived in the country and never minded the dark or the solitude. Would she now be afraid of it?

She didn't want to live that way. And she certainly didn't want to move to the city.

A thought occurred to her. "You know, Princess saved my life."

"She did more than that." Steve shot her a crooked smile. "She caught the guy who shot at you. I couldn't keep up with her. If she hadn't been there, I really think he'd have gotten away."

"Huh." She processed that information. "Maybe I should rethink my opinion of big dogs. Come to think of it, maybe it's time I thought of getting a dog. Once this is over and we no longer need to run."

But would her mother be with her? Her mom was still in serious condition. And to the best of her knowledge, she hadn't regained consciousness yet. The hospital had assured Steve they'd call to inform him of any new developments. So far, he'd received nothing.

Her mom was strong. She had to get well. But then what? She'd been hiding something from Joss, but was it enough to get her in legal trouble? She flinched away from thinking about the possible fates her mother might meet.

"A dog would help deter anyone trying to break in." Steve flipped on his left turn signal and stopped the car, pausing until a red light changed. For a moment, the steady clicks the signal made were the only sound in the car. The light switched to green, and Steve steered onto the street. The hospital loomed ahead of them.

"Do you want me to let you out under the carport? It's starting to snow again."

"Are you kidding? After the day I've had, I'm not walking anywhere without you. Not even inside that door."

"You got it."

Fortunately, there was an available parking space in the first row. Steve backed into the space with an effortlessness she envied. Joss only backed into a space if the spot next to it was empty. She was capable of backing between two cars. She just didn't like the feeling of being closed in. Deliberately trying to fit into a space that way made her sweat. So, she didn't do it—ever. But she appreciated his skill.

After shutting off the engine, Steve left the car and strode around to her side. By the time he was at her door, she'd already opened it. He frowned at her. "Sorry. I'm not used to someone opening my door for me."

"It's fine. Let's not linger."

In the hospital, it was much as she'd suspected. Her mother had been moved to a private room and a security guard was standing outside the door. He stood aside so they could enter, then promptly shut the door behind them. Joss heaved a sigh. At least everyone was taking her mother's safety seriously.

It was heartbreaking to sit at the bedside of the woman who'd raised her. There was no sign that Linda Graham was aware of anything happening around her. Joss took one of her hands. They'd never seemed frail...until now.

"Please wake up, Mom. I don't understand what's happening. Nothing makes sense."

A hand landed on her shoulder. She jumped. She'd been so absorbed by the collapse of her world, she'd forgotten Steve was in the room with her. The warmth of his hand settled her fears a bit. The temptation to close her eyes and lean against his side to absorb some of his strength startled her. She had never leaned on anyone outside of her mother. She wasn't about to start now. Straightening in her seat, she gave him a smile to thank him.

His hand slipped off her shoulder and immediately she wanted it back. She seemed so cold without that small comforting touch. Ridiculous.

"We'll come back tomorrow, Joss. Visiting hours are done."

"Can't I stay here with her? I can't go back to my house. Not after today."

He shook his head. "The chief has booked you a room at the Plain and Simple Bed-and-Breakfast. I'll be there with you, in the next room. We'll be in town, close to the police station and close to the hospital."

She tilted her head, her forehead furrowed. "Why do you need to stay there? It's not like you live in another town."

"The chief wants someone to guard you at all times. I will stand guard for a few hours, then an officer will spell me while I sleep. In the morning, we'll head out right after breakfast."

She wasn't going to argue. She'd been attacked twice in the same day. If they were taking extraordinary measures to protect her, she'd go along with it and try not to feel guilty for monopolizing so many of their resources.

Steve held a quick conference with the officer guarding the door before they departed. "You seemed so serious when you were talking to the guard. Is there anything specific you're worried about?"

Her stomach knotted. What else would go wrong?

"Not really. I just wanted to remind him of the severity of the situation." He peered down at her. "Before I became a sergeant, I had guard duty once. I made the mistake of making a flippant comment. And I was chastised for it, though politely. Taking care of your mother is more than his job. At this moment, until he's relieved, it's his mission and his sole purpose."

Wow. Knowing he felt so strongly eased her guilt.

It was eight thirty by the time they arrived at the Plain and Simple Bed-and-Breakfast. Steve had stopped and picked up a pizza and some bottled waters along the way. He set the box on a table in her room and lifted the top of the box to reveal the cheesy goodness inside. The aroma of the hot cheese-and-pepperoni pie wafted up and tickled her nose. Joss's stomach grumbled. Steve grinned. He placed a slice on a plate and handed it to her before snatching one for himself.

"Sorry. I haven't eaten since breakfast."

Steve's hand halted two inches from his mouth, a slice hanging over his fingers. His brows knit together. "I never realized. I should have—"

She waved his apology aside and bit into her dinner, rolling her eyes in appreciation at the tangy taste of the sauce. "No worries. We've had more important issues today."

And like that, the light mood dissipated.

"Yeah, we did." Steve chewed slowly. "Tomorrow will be busy. We should get some rest and get up early. I want to be at the station around eight. Will that work for you?"

"It will." The earlier the better. She was ready to leave the fear behind and get on with her life. If only they could catch who was after her.

Steve left a few minutes later after reminding her to lock her door. Not only did she lock it, but she also put a chair under the doorknob. If Steve needed to get in, they had a connecting door between their rooms.

Joss was too edgy to sleep immediately. She strolled around the room, picking up items idly. An appealing chair sat next to the single window in the room. A charming Amish rag doll was strategically placed there. Scooping up the doll, she flopped down in the chair and stretched her legs in front of her, crossing her ankles. It was a comfortable chair. She snuggled deeper into it.

Holding the doll in both hands, she smiled. It was a typical Amish toy. Dark blue dress, black apron and a crisp little prayer *kapp* on the empty face. The longer she stared at the innocent toy, however, the weirder she felt. Her smile dripped from her face.

She'd never, in her memory, touched one of these dolls, much less held one. But a small voice inside her soul remembered doing exactly that. She couldn't claim amnesia. Nor had she played with any Amish children in her life, although she'd seen them around.

Something wasn't adding up. In her heart, she knew this feeling of déjà vu was connected to all the things her mother never told her.

Secrets she needed to know to stay alive.

SIX

"Well, that was a waste of time." Joss slipped past Steve and climbed into his cruiser. They'd spent the entire morning at the police station, poring over the digital database. Her eyes had been glued to a screen so long they ached and she'd developed a slight headache. Although she'd found the man who'd killed Hal, the one she really wanted to find, the evil man who'd shot her mother, she'd not seen.

"It's okay. Just because you didn't see him today, doesn't mean we won't find him." Steve got in and handed her a bottle of water before he reached into the console area and found a bottle of ibuprofen. He handed it over to her without comment then started the ignition.

Touched, she smiled. "How did you know I had a headache?"

"I saw you rubbing your temples earlier." He shrugged. "I always keep bottled water in the back and pain relievers on hand. You never know when you'll need them."

"You're not wrong. Thanks."

She swallowed two tablets and took an extra sip of water before twisting the cap back on the bottle. "So, what's our plan for the day?"

"Well, Francesca, our forensic artist, won't be available until Monday. Which means I need to focus my attention on a different angle of the investigation." He hesitated. "I need to search your house. The chief suggested I drop you off at the hospital…"

She shook her head. "No, I need to help. You don't know my mom. She had secret hiding places, I'm not even supposed to know about them. But I was always too curious for my own good."

He laughed. "Fine. But I was going to take you anyways. I told the chief that this morning."

She nodded. That was as it should be. It was hard to explain. She'd only known him since yesterday, but she felt safer when he was by her side. Added to that, Joss needed to know what was going on. What her mom had been hiding. She recalled her intuition the night before, that she'd held an Amish doll before, even though she couldn't remember ever having done so.

Joss didn't like secrets.

They arrived at her house a few minutes before eleven. Steve halted the cruiser in the exact spot her mother usually parked. Joss's throat swelled. She cleared it a few times. When she was in control, she twisted a bit and met Steve's concerned gaze.

"Joss, are you sure you're okay to do this?"

She bit her lip, her gaze jerking toward the home she'd lived in for the past decade. "I have to. It looks so beautiful, you know? All the trees and the pristine snow. I'd forgotten how often we'd leave in the wee hours of the morning. But I need to know what part of my life was real and what part was a lie."

He shifted in his seat, moving so he was facing her. "I don't know what we'll find."

"I know that. Thank you for not telling me I'm overreacting."

He frowned, his gaze scanning the horizon. "Sometimes we know in our gut something is wrong. If we don't try to find out what, we might regret it. But, yeah, there are moments when we need to be logical."

Whoa. She heard more than a kernel of experience there. What had happened to him? She shied away from the question. He deserved his privacy. If he ever decided to tell her more, she'd listen, but she'd not press for more information than he was ready to share.

"Let's do this." She firmed her lips.

He stared at her for about three seconds. Then he nodded and opened his door. She met him at the front of the cruiser. Together, they silently tromped up the steps. It seemed odd to see them unshoveled. That had always been Joss's job, but she hadn't slept there last night.

She paused, one foot hovering on the edge of the top step.

"What?"

She shook her head. "Just an odd thought. I can't remember the last time I spent a night away from my mom. It always bothered her when I was gone. She has this app on her phone. One that tells her where I am at all times. I often tease her about being overprotective."

She climbed the top step and rifled through her purse in search of her keys. At her side, Steve scanned the tree line. Her fingers touched her key ring.

"Aha!" She pulled it out with a flourish and unlocked the door.

Once inside, Steve pushed the door closed behind them and locked it. "Hold on. Let me check to make sure the house is safe."

She opened her mouth to agree, but he'd already had his gun out and was off on his mission.

While he searched, she went into the kitchen and made herself some coffee, a familiar task that made her feel a little like her old self. When he came back, she was already sipping a steaming mug with a healthy dose of French vanilla cream and artificial sweetener. "Want some?"

"Maybe later."

She took one last sip and set her mug on the counter. "Where should we search first?"

"Your mom's room, I'd guess. We're looking for that note or any clues as to why she was targeted."

"This way." She led him up the stairs to the room her mom had used the entire time they'd lived there. She flung the door open. The space was the same as it had been the last time she'd been there, right before they'd fled. But something felt off. "I feel like something's wrong."

She shuddered. The spot between her shoulder blades tingled.

"Joss?"

"It's nothing. You know the saying someone just walked over my grave? I feel like that. Like I'm being spied on."

He frowned and stepped closer to her. His

warmth sent her pulse fluttering for another reason altogether. "It's probably nerves from being back here where it started. Let's do this and get out of here."

He'd get no argument from her.

"Mom likes to hide things in several spots." She reached into the closet and shoved all the dresses aside. A small safe was snuggled into the back. It was only about a foot high.

"What's the combination?"

She lifted both hands to the height of her shoulders. "I have no clue. I found it here several years ago while snooping around. It was during my rebel phase."

"Well, a safe isn't unusual. Many people have them."

"True. I'm curious what's in there, though." She shrugged. "I wonder..." She tapped out a four-digit code. Her birthday. She didn't expect it to work. When she heard a distinct click, she gasped. "I can't believe that did the trick!"

Now that it worked, though, she found herself reluctant to open it. Steeling herself, she took hold of the knob and swung the door open. Inside, a single garment bag was stuffed. She carefully lifted it out.

"I've never seen this before." Unzipping the bag, she spread the contents on her mother's bed. A plain blue dress, obviously made for an Amish child. A small prayer *kapp*. And an Amish doll that showed considerable wear. As if a young girl carried it around with her. Shivering, she wrapped her arms around herself.

Steve brushed her arm. "You've gone pale."

She lifted her eyes to his face. "Last night, at the bed-and-breakfast, I saw an Amish doll in my room, and I felt like it was familiar. Which was ridiculous because I'd never touched one before. Except—" she touched the apron on the small doll "—I think I have. Steve, I think this dress and doll were mine. I have no memory of them, and they're so small, I must have been only two or so, but why else would she have them?"

His silence spoke louder than any response he could have had.

What had her mother done?

What exactly had Linda Graham gotten herself into? And how did Joss fit into all of it?

Steve stared at the dress and the doll. He had to admit, it was hard to imagine why she'd have these items hidden in a safe in the back of her closet. It was unlikely she'd adopted Joss privately from an Amish woman. That wouldn't explain the frequent moves. The only explanation that made sense to him, and he really didn't want to think it, was that Linda Graham had abducted a child.

He stole a peek at Joss. Her expression revealed how devastated she was feeling. That motivated him to action.

"Put it all back in the garment bag."

She lifted her face to his, her brows furrowed. "What do you plan to do with it?"

The trust shining from those eyes pierced him. He had to swallow before he could respond to her question.

"It's most likely evidence. I have a hunch this is somehow going to tie in to what's been going on. Let's bring it in."

She shoved the dress, *kapp* and doll into the garment bag so fast it was obvious she wanted them out of her sight. Then she all but threw the bag at him.

"You take them." She'd been so controlled since he'd met her yesterday, it shocked him to see her so rattled. He took the bag casually, not letting on that he saw how staggered she had been at the discovery.

She laughed, a brittle, broken sound. When she stumbled toward the dresser, he twisted his head to follow her movements. There was nothing he could say to heal the wound in her heart. A glint out of the corner of his eye caught his attention. Steve's head whipped toward the window. A flash of light flared, then it was gone.

Almost like the glare of the sun reflecting off something metallic.

"Get down!" Steve lurched at Joss. She whirled to face him. "Down! Sniper in the trees."

She dropped beside the bed. He fell at her side. A bullet smashed through the window. It hit the mirror on the opposite side of the room. The glass shattered and shards scattered across the hard wood floor.

"Stay here!" Steve told her. "I'm going after him."

"Steve!"

"I have to go now, Joss. While we know where the sniper is. Call 911. Tell them what's happened and don't hang up until backup arrives."

He fled down the steps and ran to the back door. This part of the house was even with the slope of the landscape, so he didn't have to deal with icy steps. He leapt out the door, letting it bang closed behind him. Steve raced toward the edge of the property. The shooter had come from beyond the metal toolshed. Possibly in a tree, as he'd hit the second-floor window.

The pager hooked to his belt sprang to life. The dispatcher issued an active shooting announcement, then she proceeded to spit out a call for police backup to Joss's address. After that, she asked for an ambulance and more emergency units to be on call. Within moments, Steve knew, the road would be barricaded and police would swarm the area, outfitted in Kevlar vests and carrying various weapons. No one underestimated the danger of a shooter on the loose.

Was this the same man who'd shot Linda, or was there yet another shooter out there, intent on ending Joss's life?

A bullet whizzed by and lodged in the side of the shed, a mere six inches from where his head had been seconds ago. Steve ducked down and used an obliging tree to take cover. He spun around the tree and saw a shape fifty feet away. He aimed and fired, then withdrew. Within seconds, another bullet hit the side of the tree.

This guy wasn't too bright. Surely, he had to know that backup was on the way. Maybe he'd been paid for proof of her death, or maybe he'd been threatened if he failed a second time. Whatever the reason, Steve wasn't going to give him the opportunity to succeed in his quest. He was going down. Steve hardened his jaw and dashed from his cover, charging toward the sniper's hiding place.

The sniper leaned out of his cover. Steve's gun was ready. He fired but kept his momentum going.

A satisfying yelp echoed through the air. He'd gotten him.

Slowing, he marched forward, his gun remaining aloft. "Police. Hands up. Come out where I can see you."

Instead of obeying, the man scrambled away, heading deeper into the trees. Steve had no difficulty following his trail. The sniper made enough noise to wake a hibernating bear.

Something wasn't right. Anyone who did any sort of hunting, animal or human, knew better than to carry on or make that kind of racket. Steve put on a burst of speed and rushed his prey.

The shooter spotted him advancing and bolted, dropping his rifle in the process.

That's when Steve knew. It was a trap. There was no way he'd leave his weapon behind. Steve caught him.

"You fool." The man spat the words out. "You got me, but you left your girl back there undefended."

Even as unease uncurled in his belly, he heard the sirens. The backup had arrived.

His radio crackled. "Sergeant Beck, we're on the scene."

"Officer Zilhaver, Miss Graham is inside the house. I think the sniper was a decoy. Check on her safety. I have the shooter under control."

While he waited, he cuffed his sniper, patted him down and searched for more weapons. There were none to be found. Then he grabbed the gun and frog-marched the man back toward the house. At this point, all he wanted was to assure himself that Joss was safe. His jaw ached from clenching his teeth so tight. He couldn't remember the last time he'd been so angry.

"She's in the house, Sergeant." Zilhaver's voice was broken up over the static, but his words were clear enough. Steve unclenched his teeth. Opening his mouth slightly, he moved his jaw back and forth, working out the ache.

Officer Zilhaver's cruiser purred in the driveway. The man himself stood in front of the vehicle, arms crossed over his broad chest. He squinted at them as Steve pushed the sniper the last few yards.

"You read him his rights?"

"Sure did. While we were walking. He's all yours."

Zilhaver shoved the man toward the car. "I'll

bring him in for you, then we can get his statement."

"We'll interview him at the station." Steve kept his voice low. "Hopefully, he'll flip on the ringleader. I know he's nothing more than a hired hand. Someone else ordered these shootings."

It was the only thing that made sense.

Officer Zilhaver stomped around the side of the car and opened the back door to his cruiser. Steve backed away from him, already set to return to the house and check on Joss. Zilhaver put his hands on the sniper's head, intent on easing him down into the back seat so he could be transported to the police station and properly booked.

The sniper suddenly gulped. "I don't want to die this way."

What? The hair stood on the back of Steve's neck. That sounded like—

Horror hit him. Steve lurched forward. "Tim—"

A blast of heat hurled him to the ground. Pain seared his neck.

Joss.

Everything went black.

SEVEN

Joss heard an explosion and sprang to her feet, only one thought on her mind. "Steve!"

What if something had happened to him? He'd been gone so long. All his warnings to remain where she was vanished from her mind. Scrambling to the door, she left the bag he'd dropped when he'd run out and she fumbled with the doorknob. Once the door was open, she fled her mother's room and launched herself down the steps, intent on reaching Steve quickly.

He might be hurt. She refused to think it could be worse than that.

At the bottom of the steps, she paused. Red and blue lights flashed outside, splashing the crisp cream walls of her house with shards of brightness like a disco ball. She heard the wails of another emergency vehicle. She recognized the sound of an ambulance. And then the wail of a fire truck.

The dispatcher must have had them on standby. They never could have arrived so fast if they were coming on the first call. The best she'd expect from the volunteer fire department was fifteen minutes. Not even five had passed since the explosion.

Determined, she bounded toward the front door.

A meaty hand hooked her elbow and yanked her back. She swung around and found herself facing a complete stranger. A stranger with the coldest eyes she'd ever seen. She read her death in those eyes and chills worked their way up her spine.

He might have been handsome, in a vague, unmemorable way, if it weren't for the snarl on his face. "Where's Emily?"

Emily? Joss blinked at the vicious stranger. "I don't know any Em—"

He shook her. Her words broke off as her head wobbled on her neck.

"Don't play games with me. I know who you are, don't think I don't. She's kept you hidden all these years. But it's her I want. You don't have to get hurt."

Linda. He wanted her mom, except he was

calling her Emily, not Linda. She didn't believe he'd let her go. Not for an instant. He planned for both of them to die. But why?

"I can't. Please. I don't know any Emily."

She had to keep him from guessing the truth. And she had to find a way to escape from him. Steve. What had happened to Steve? Unthinking, her eyes flashed to the front door. The commotion, voices yelling and orders flying, came through the door in a muffled cacophony.

"Your cop is dead. You can't do anything for him."

Grief hit her like a load of cement bricks had been dropped on her head. She fought her way through it. He might be wrong. Even if he wasn't, she couldn't give up. She snatched her arm from his painful grasp. Inching away from him, she rubbed her elbow.

Think, Joss, think. There had to be a way to outsmart him and make her escape. Especially with all the cops and emergency responders outside. All she needed was enough time to alert them.

She could scream—

"Open your mouth and you'll be dead before they can save you. And whoever comes in to play hero will follow you to the morgue."

She bit her lip, forcing her scream back. She

wouldn't be the cause of any more deaths. Not like Hal. Or Steve?

Her mind circled around to what he said—that she'd been hidden. Why? What possible reason could she have for concealing Joss from him? Joss's stomach curdled. This evil man was not her father. She'd know if he were, wouldn't she?

He reached out and yanked her to him again. "Enough. I know you know where she is and how to get to her. Once I get you away from here, you'll talk."

He smirked at the front door. "All is going according to my plan."

The sniper. She swayed as the blood rushed from her head. The man shooting through the window had missed her on purpose. Steve had chased him, but it was all part of the plot to get her alone. Now, she struggled in earnest, fighting and clawing to break free. One hand managed to scrape down his cheek. Not enough to draw blood, but enough to cause him to flinch back from her perfectly manicured short and sporty nails.

The grip on her arm loosened. Tugging free again, she spun and dashed for the back door.

He caught her. She saw the hand coming but didn't have time to duck before he slapped her.

Joss's head whipped to the side. Forgetting her promise to remain quiet, Joss cried out in pain.

"You shouldn't have done that. I don't need you." He thrust his face close to hers. "You could have gotten away, but now—"

The front doorknob jiggled. Something slammed against it.

Cursing, the man dropped her arm, lunged through the house and fled out the back door. Joss swayed as the adrenaline running through her veins crashed. The front door burst open. Steve raced inside, dried blood splattered on his right cheek and temple, fury deep in his dark eyes.

"Steve! I thought you were dead!" she croaked out and then broke into loud sobs.

Very gently, he hefted her into his arms and carried her to the sofa nestled on the opposite side of the room. He lowered her down, then joined her. Joss buried her face in his shoulder, striving to get herself under control. She had to tell him what the stranger had said.

Steve's hand brushed her head. She quieted. When a hiccup erupted, she pulled back, allowing her long hair to block her blushing face from view.

So much for the image of self-control she tried to maintain.

"Joss, are you all right? Did he hurt you?"

Shaking her hair away from her face, she scanned him for any other signs of injury. "I'm fine."

He touched her sore cheek, his jaw hardening. "He hit you."

"Yeah, but nothing else. Steve, the shooter was a trap."

He sighed heavily. "I know. The man said as much when I caught him."

"Did he confess? Do you know who that man was?"

Silence descended for three heartbeats.

"The shooter had a hidden explosive on him. I didn't find it when I frisked him."

"A bomb!"

He nodded. "Yeah. It went off and took him out. He never had a chance." He swallowed. "Tim Zilhaver's dead, too."

Oh, no. Tears blinded her again. She remembered the exuberant officer. "I'm so sorry."

"He was a friend." He paused. "I think the shooter was an unwilling participant. Before the explosive went off, he said he didn't want to die. I think the bomb was another decoy. It must have been set off by remote control. The bomb squad is on its way."

She touched his hand. There was nothing

she could say to remove the hurt he'd suffered. She wanted him to know he wasn't alone. He flipped his hand over and clasped her fingers, squeezing them briefly. The warmth of his palm against hers seared through her.

When he dropped her hand, she didn't protest. Allowing the attraction simmering between them to blossom would not be smart. She shouldn't encourage it.

Joss cleared her throat. "He was searching for 'Emily.' And he claimed she'd been hiding me. She must have changed her name to Linda at some point."

"It fits. If Linda stole you, or if she was part of a group that did such things, maybe she chickened out. Or maybe she decided to keep you. Such things have happened before."

Her breath hitched. They were seriously considering the theory that she, Joss Graham, was in fact a baby snatched from her biological parents. That somewhere out there she had another family.

How much more could she take before she broke completely?

He was shocked to the core by Tim's death coming so soon after Hal's. And he didn't like the haunted expression crossing Joss's face. She looked as lost as he felt. He wanted to put his arms around her again but forced himself to stand instead. Holding her had been a mistake.

"Sergeant Beck." Kathy's soft voice interrupted the moment.

He pivoted on his heel, grateful for the reprieve. Shoving his hands into his pockets, he moved over to where she hovered in the doorway, sorrow darkening her gaze. He wasn't prepared for her to grab him in a quick hug. He patted her shoulder. She and Zilhaver had been friends as well. In fact, Kathy had mentored the younger officer when he first joined as a rookie straight from the academy, as green as they came. She had to be hurting.

They both cleared their throats and separated. They had a job to do. Kathy swiped her sleeve across her face. When she glanced at him again, her face was pale, but dry.

"The bomb squad's here. They want to talk with you."

He nodded, dreading the coming interview. He started toward the door, then paused. "Kath. Do me a favor? Stay with Joss?"

Kathy waved him away. "I won't budge until you return."

Steve hurried outside. A crystalline snowflake hit his uninjured cheek, melting on contact. Great. Now he'd have to deal with falling snow. Pounding down the steps, he met up with the woman sent over from the Hazardous Devices Unit, also known as the bomb squad.

"Sergeant." She ducked her head.

"Lieutenant."

The pleasantries done, she briefed him on what she'd need to do. "Can you give me a rundown of what occurred here today?"

Steve sucked in a painful breath. He could do this. Focusing his attention on a spot over her shoulder, he recited the events of the past hour and a half as succinctly as possible. She asked several brisk questions, then took over the conversation.

"My team will require access to the entire scene. Since the second perp was in the house, it's fair to assume the device was tripped from there. You said you frisked the first perp?"

He swallowed the resentment that surged. She was doing her job, not questioning his performance. His distress over Tim's death was affecting his perspective.

"Yes, ma'am. He had no weapons or wires on him. Nothing that resembled an explosive."

She nodded. "I believe you, Sergeant. We'll take it from here."

He escaped before they could ask anything

else. Puffing out a relieved breath, he spun around and headed back to the house—then paused. He couldn't face Joss yet. His emotions were still going haywire. The chief. He'd call the chief.

Wheeling away from the house, he moved beyond the crime scene tape and met with Officer Hansen's stark expression for a moment. Working on your partner's murder scene had to be brutal.

The chief already knew the pertinent details when he checked in. "Do you need time off, Steve?"

It was a sure sign of the seriousness of the situation when Chief Spencer referred to an officer on duty by their first name.

"I'd prefer to continue working, Chief. At least until we have this perp. Then I can take time off if I need it."

The chief grunted. "I can't say I'm sorry to hear it. We're stretched thin, Steve. I need you at your best, but I don't know how we'd cover all shifts on this one if you took time now."

"I wouldn't want your job," Steve mused, eliciting a surprised chuckle tinged with bitterness.

"Honestly? On days like today, I don't much want my job either. Tell me if anything new develops."

"Will do."

Steve clicked the end button on his phone and headed back to the house. It was only one in the afternoon. He should make sure Joss ate, although he had no appetite himself. Clumping up the steps, he walked into the house and was hit with a wave of delicious aromas wafting out from the kitchen. Following his nose, he found Joss stirring ingredients in a skillet while Kathy sat at a chair at the table.

"What's going on?"

"She insisted," Kathy said with a shrug.

Joss flipped her dark hair over a shoulder. Even distressed, she was lovely in her dark blue jeans, casual deep blue blouse and the long open cream cardigan. He blinked. Now was not the time for such thoughts.

"Stir-fry," she answered. "I know you're probably not hungry, and I'm not sure how much I can choke down, but cooking soothes me when I'm upset, and you all need something to eat."

He was touched by how she wanted to do something to comfort them, and he wouldn't turn down a home-cooked meal, especially knowing it might help her deal with the nightmarish situation they'd found themselves in. "What can I do to help?"

She glanced around, frowning while perusing the countertops and stove. "Nothing really. You can get out plates and silverware."

It was an odd feeling, eating while the bomb squad worked directly outside the door. He managed to swallow a few bites. Mostly, he pushed the food around on his plate. So did Joss. Kathy, he noticed, ate better. He was glad.

Kathy helped clean up the dishes and put the leftovers in the refrigerator. A knock on the door stopped all motion. Steve handed Joss the towel he'd been drying the dishes with. He let the team leader for the bomb squad inside.

While Steve greeted the bomb squad leader, Joss's phone rang. She crossed to the living room to answer it. Wary, Steve placed himself next to the island at the edge of the kitchen. He had a clear view of Joss from there, as well as the length of the kitchen, depending on which way he was looking. No one could get past without him noticing. Switching his stare back to the bomb squad leader, he nodded.

She didn't keep them waiting. "Your first perp was wearing an explosive wired into his watch. Best we can figure, it was a time-delay device."

"Why would he agree to wear such a thing?"

Steve asked. The man had definitely known he was wearing a rigged device.

The team leader shrugged. "He might have had no choice. You don't know what his boss had on him."

"I really want to catch this creep," Kathy growled.

"You and me both," Steve agreed. "We need to learn more about him. Maybe when Linda Graham wakes up, we'll get some answers."

"That might happen sooner than you thought," Joss said, holding up her phone.

"What do you mean?"

"That was the hospital. My mom woke up ten minutes ago."

Steve bounded over to her. "Does she remember what happened?"

She shrugged. "I don't know. But we have to go talk to her. She's the only one who really knows what's going on."

He didn't argue.

"You two go." Kathy flicked her hands at them. "I'll take care of everything on this end."

"Hold on." Joss ran to the stairs and disappeared from view. He heard her feet stamping on the hard wood floors. When she returned, the garment bag he'd left behind when he'd chased the decoy sniper dangled from her fingers. "We might as well ask her about this, too."

Steve avoided peering at the mess that had been Tim's car on the way to his cruiser. Joss gaped for a couple of seconds before gulping and turning away.

Steve held the passenger door open for her. She hopped in quickly, avoiding looking back. He loped around and got in the driver's side. Instead of starting the engine, however, he turned to her.

"I'm thinking we need to exchange phone numbers. I don't like the thought of not being able to get in touch with you if something happens."

She nodded and quietly gave him her number. He added it to his device, then sent her a text. While she updated her contacts to include him, he started the cruiser and left her driveway.

The ride to the hospital was silent. Steve had too much running through his mind to keep up his side of a conversation. Grief and anger vied for control of his mind.

Lord, help me. I need Your grace to get past my anger and catch this guy.

"Amen," Joss whispered.

He jerked his head in her direction. He hadn't intended to pray out loud.

Her lips tilted up at the corners. "I was praying, too. Actually, my prayer was similar. I need to work past my emotions, as well. But God can do this, Steve."

He sighed. "I know. But I need to get myself out of His way. I tend to think I have more control of the world around me than I do."

She snorted. "Yeah, I know how that goes."

Her eyes slipped to the bag at her feet. She must have felt like she had no control over her life. She didn't even know who she really was. He couldn't imagine how terrifying that would be.

Once inside the hospital, they walked the familiar route to Linda Graham's room. The guard glanced at them and moved aside. Joss knocked once before opening the door and popping her head inside.

"Mom." A wealth of love and relief was sunk into that one word.

"Josslyn," he heard the woman murmur.

Joss pushed the door the rest of the way open and motioned for him to come in with her. As if he planned to wait outside. He let her go in first, then quietly shut the door behind them. The woman on the bed observed him keenly.

"Mom, this is Sergeant Steve Beck. He saved us. And he's saved my life several times since your wreck."

Was that only yesterday?

The woman on the bed gasped, her hands clasped together on her chest. "Joss? What's happened?"

"Miss Graham." Steve approached the bed. He didn't want to leave the explanation to Joss. "You were shot while leaving your home. Your car crashed. The man who shot you escaped. Since then, he's hired someone to shoot at least one more person and had two more killed. He tried to kidnap Joss this afternoon. He got away, unfortunately."

Linda's face blanched. He feared she'd pass out again.

"Josslyn, you have to run!"

Joss shook her head, her lips pressed together in a hard line. "No. I will not run. Mom, who is he? Why was he looking for 'Emily'?" She ignored her mother's gasp and plopped the garment bag on the bed. "And why was this in the safe in your closet?"

Her mom's jaw dropped open, but no sound emerged. Steve's patience dwindled every second that passed.

Joss leaned closer and opened the bag. She

lifted out the worn Amish doll. "I know this doll. Mom, why do I remember this?"

Bowing her head, Linda's tears streamed down her cheeks. In spite of himself, pity moved Steve's heart. She might have been behind this, but his gut told him her guilt and sorrow were genuine.

"You remember it because it was yours." Her tortured gaze lifted to her daughter's face. "I was 'Emily' a long time ago. That doll, and the dress and bonnet, were yours. You had them when we met."

"'Met'?" Joss's voice was little more than a whisper. Steve grabbed the chair near the bed and slid it to Joss. He gently clasped her arm and assisted her as she sat. Her glance never left the other woman's face. When he tried to step away, her hand slid into his and held on tight. "What do you mean, 'when we met'?"

She already knew. Steve was certain of it.

"Twenty-two years ago, you were an Amish child, stolen from your home. I intended to return you to your family, but it was never safe. Finally, I decided to keep you."

EIGHT

She was stolen from an Amish family.

Joss couldn't think. The shock of Linda's—or Emily's—statement had her gasping. Her mind was unable to process what the woman said. Emily stared at her, pleading with her eyes for her to understand.

She slumped against the back of the chair, her heart pounding in her ears.

A nurse interrupted the discussion. She smiled at Emily and checked her IV. Then she adjusted her medicines. Joss bit her lip. She knew what that meant. They only had a few minutes before her mother was out again.

"Mom." She paused. How could she call this woman mom? Somewhere, the woman who'd given birth to her lived. Had her parents searched for her? Did they give her up for dead? Or were they still trying to find her?

No. She stared into Emily's eyes. No matter what else she'd done, Emily had raised her and loved her. You could not make that kind of affection up. Whatever she'd done, Joss owed her the gift of letting her explain, without judgment. "Mom, please tell me what happened. Who is after you?"

Emily's head sank into the pillow. Her lids drifted closed. "My real name is Emily. The man searching for me is my husband, Kevin. Find my journal, Joss. I kept track…" Her voice petered out for a moment. For a second, Joss thought she was under. Then Emily stirred again. "Joss. My phone. Take it. 0329."

"0329?" She leaned closer. "Mom? Is that your password? Does it mean anything?"

"The day you were taken. By my husband."

Her husband. But not Joss's father. That was the one silver lining. At least she had no relation to that man. She shivered at the memory of his cold eyes. Steve's hand tightened on hers. She'd forgotten that she'd clutched his hand in her distress. Flushing, she slid her fingers out of his.

Glancing at him under her lashes, she murmured a quiet thanks before returning her attention back to the woman on the bed.

"Why were you running from him?"

Emily didn't answer. She had fallen back to

sleep. It would be useless trying to talk further. Joss tilted her head back and met his gaze. "She'll sleep for a few hours. The medication."

Steve blew out a hard breath. "Great. Just when we were starting to get some answers."

Joss sighed. "I apologize. I'm familiar with these medications. I should have asked the nurse to delay the pain meds. I was just too distraught to think of it."

Steve placed a warm hand on her shoulder and gave a gentle squeeze. "You've got nothing to apologize for."

He removed his hand and jammed it into his coat pocket.

She rubbed her hands over her face. "I didn't see a journal when we were at the house. In fact, I don't recall ever seeing a journal. Do you think she knew what she was saying?"

Steve helped her to her feet. "You'd know better than me about how the meds might affect her. But I think we need to go on the assumption that there is a journal. Any idea where else she might have hidden something like that?"

"I thought we searched the house pretty thoroughly. I'll need to think about this."

"Hey, she told you to grab her phone. Maybe there's something on there that will help you."

Joss looked around. "I don't see her phone."

"It's in evidence. I'll get the chief to clear it. I'm sure he'll okay it, since it's part of the investigation."

Joss allowed him to hold the door open for her, then stepped into the hall with him. She smiled politely at the guard while he was closing the door to the room.

"Any changes, let me know," Steve instructed the guard.

Joss wandered a few feet to the elevator and waited for him to catch up. When he met her, his face was set in troubled lines. He ushered her into the elevator and jabbed the button for the first floor.

She waited until they had left the hospital and were striding through the light snow to the car before she spoke. "What are we going to do?"

He walked to her door and opened it for her. He reached out and brushed a snowflake from her cheek. She felt the heat of his fingers down to her toes. "Your mom didn't give as much information as I'd like. Emily and Kevin are fairly common names. But she did give us a date. March 29th. We have to assume she wasn't sure of your birth year. But maybe we can get close enough."

She blinked at him. "Close enough for what?"

He gave her a sad smile. "To find your birth family."

Joss nearly fell into her seat. Did she want to find her birth family? Part of her hungered to meet them, to know about the people she came from. The other part worried. What if they demanded more than she could give? The last thing she wanted was to cause them more pain. But there was no way she could ever be a full part of their family again. She didn't know that much about Amish culture, but she didn't think she'd ever belong there.

Steve closed her door and strode around the front of the vehicle. Once he was settled in his seat, he started the engine. "Don't fret so much. We've come too far not to search. And Joss?"

"Yes?" She lifted her gaze to his. Her breath stalled at the tenderness on his face.

"They need to know."

"But so suddenly? Shouldn't we wait until we've found the journal and you've closed the case?"

"No." There was no hesitation. "I lost my family when I was fifteen. My father was a closet drunk. When I was barely fifteen, my family went out. My dad was in a mood. I had smelled the alcohol on his breath, but I didn't try hard enough to stop him. He wasn't obviously under the influence. But I knew he shouldn't drive. When they left, I stayed home. I was supposed to go, but I had other plans. An hour later, the police knocked on the door. All of them, my parents and my ten-year-old twin sisters, all of them were gone."

Her heart hammered in her chest. "Oh, wow. Steve, that's awful."

How did one cope with such devastation? He shrugged it off, but his shoulders were tense. "I never talk of this. Not sure why I'm telling you. But if someone told me there was a possibility a family member I lost was still alive, I would be so overjoyed, I wouldn't care about anything except having them back in my life."

"So…" She said the words slowly, thinking them through as she spoke. "I should meet them for their sake, not mine."

"Exactly." He sent a smile her way. The sadness in the curve of his lower lip nearly rent her already wounded heart in two.

"I guess you have a point." She twisted to stare out the window. "I wonder if I have any brothers or sisters. I'd always wanted a sibling."

"Well, hopefully, we'll be able to find out."

She turned her head back to look at him.

He rubbed his hand along his jaw. "First, I

want to know where we should start searching. You said you'd moved around a lot."

"Yeah." She sat up straighter in her seat. "How many states have Amish communities?"

He shook his head. "I haven't a clue. But I do know that the color and cut of the dress you came with, and the prayer *kapp* might help us narrow it down a little bit. And we can look up records on kidnappings around the time of your birth."

Joss laid her head on the headrest and groaned, rolling her head back and forth. "This is so frustrating! Just when I think we've made progress, you throw another obstacle in my way. Part of me wants to get it over with and locate my biological parents. Part of me wants everything to go away. And all of me wants it to happen quickly."

He patted her hand. "I'm not trying to be difficult. I'm trying to be efficient."

She tossed him her best sassy grin. "I know. I'm giving you a hard time, and I shouldn't. You've been great. But I am frustrated. Patience is not in my skill set."

"Huh. I get it. Want those answers yesterday, do you?"

She nodded. "Yes. But that's not going to happen." She stopped smiling. "I want this to be done. I want my mom to come home and I want to live my life."

He hesitated. "Joss, about your mom…"

She sighed. "I know. No matter what she said about planning to return me, she still kept me as her own."

"She did. Why didn't she go to the police? That would have been the obvious first choice, if she really meant to give you back."

If. Joss bit her thumbnail. She didn't want to consider the implications of that statement.

Ahead of them, the lights at a railroad crossing flashed, and the arm descended. He rolled to a stop and surveyed her, his brow furrowed. "It sounds harsh, but she didn't just 'keep' you. She went through the trouble to change your name, get you illegal documentation so you could attend school and find a job. And she never told you the truth. You're what? Twenty-five?"

"I thought I was. But like you said, she might have misjudged my age."

The more he said, the darker her mood became. She barely noticed the car vibrating as a freight train clattered past.

"I'm sorry. I don't want to upset you. But this wasn't a benign accident. Her keeping you was a deliberate, well thought-out and executed plan. There will be consequences for that."

Her stomach roiled. She put a hand over her unhappy belly and breathed through her nose. She heard what he said. No matter how kind and loving she'd been, Linda-Emily wouldn't be coming home. The mother who raised her would probably spend the rest of her life in jail.

And there was nothing Joss could do to prevent it.

Steve pulled into the police station and killed the engine. Joss hadn't said a word, much less looked at him, in the past twenty minutes. He rubbed the back of his neck, guilt pricking his conscience. Everything he had said was true. Still, maybe he could have broken it to her more easily. Or picked a better time. The woman was already reeling from the discovery that her whole life was a lie.

Then he hit her by taking the only mother she'd ever known and telling her she'd never be with her again.

Talk about kicking someone when they were down.

He turned to her and opened his mouth, but then snapped it shut. What could he say? He didn't want to risk it being the wrong thing and bringing her even lower than she was at this moment. Holding in a sigh, he stepped from the cruiser. He said a quick prayer for guidance then strode to the other side. For once, she didn't meet him, but was still sitting in the car.

Cocking his head to get a better view, his lips broke into a smile. She hadn't been pouting. Joss's head was cushioned against the corner of the window, her face turned toward the glass. With every exhale, the window fogged.

She had fallen asleep.

Now, this was a quandary. If he opened the door, she'd probably fall onto the pavement. On the other hand, if he knocked on the glass, he'd freak her out. Terrifying her after all she'd survived was not a good idea.

Shaking his head at the ridiculousness of the situation, he chuckled and grabbed his cell phone and sent her a quick text. Maybe the notification sound would nudge her awake. He waited. From where he stood, he saw her phone light up in the pocket of her purse.

She didn't move.

He stood in the cold trying to figure out what to do. Finally, he sighed and gently opened the door. Easing it wider, he slid his hand in, bracing her shoulder. Joss fell forward a couple of inches, then jolted upright. She reminded him of an owl, the way she blinked up at him. He grinned into her bemused face.

"Come on, sleepy girl. Time to go into the station. It's cold out here."

She scrunched her forehead for a moment before her brow cleared and her eyes widened. "Oops. Guess I didn't get enough sleep last night."

"No problem. I'm sure the chief's waiting for us in his office." He stepped back, holding the door open so she would have enough room. Joss gathered her purse, slid the strap over her shoulder, then reached down and picked up the garment bag.

Her mouth tightened as she hefted the second item. He withheld from commenting.

Brushing her free hand through her tangled hair, she placed one foot on the paved driveway and stood up. But she moved too fast and swayed on her feet.

Steve rushed forward and steadied her. When she raised her head, the flippant comment he'd planned to make remained unsaid. Suddenly, he was completely aware of Joss in his arms, not as a case he was working, but as a beautiful young woman.

It would be so easy to lean down and kiss her.

He searched her face. She seemed as caught in the moment as he was.

The sudden clack of hooves hitting the street jerked him back to reality. An Amish buggy rolled by, three young children staring at him from the back window. He couldn't kiss her. Lovely as she was, Josslyn Graham was part of a case. A complicated one. The woman didn't even know who she was and she had someone out to kill her. The last thing she needed in her life was the added stress of a romance.

Especially one with a sergeant who had commitment issues of his own. For Steve Beck knew he was too broken. He had little to offer anyone. No matter how strong they were. Or beautiful. Or compassionate. Joss was an amazing woman. She just wasn't the woman for him. Or rather, a broken man like him wasn't the man for her.

He ignored the ache in his chest and put some space between them. "Come on."

He'd confused her with his quickly changed mood. He couldn't help it. He needed to remind himself to keep his distance from her. If not physically, at least emotionally. Otherwise, he'd break both their hearts.

They'd both had enough of that in their lives.

Walking into the station, Steve was careful to keep at least a foot between them. Joss kept sending him questioning glances. He pretended not to notice. Once inside, he buzzed them in to the main part of the station and led her past the officers' desks to Chief Spencer's office. The door was open and the chief was at his desk. Out of respect, Steve rapped on the door twice.

"Sergeant Beck. Miss Graham. Please come in." Although the chief smiled, it was forced.

Steve moved aside for Joss to proceed into the simply furnished office. He and Joss both took seats in the chairs across from the chief's desk.

"Chief, I'm sorry about Tim. If I'd realized it was a trap sooner—"

The chief cut him off. "I don't blame you for Officer Zilhaver's death, Steve, and neither should you. You did your job. You knew when you took your oath it might cost you. As did Tim. He was a fine officer. He knew what he was doing. Someone else is responsible for his death. And it's not anyone sitting in this room."

That got his attention. Did Joss think she was responsible? He peeked at her and glimpsed the guilt before it slid off her face.

"If I'm not guilty, you definitely aren't," he told her.

The chief sighed and clasped his hands together on his desk. "I've just had the awful task of informing Tim's mother and fiancée of his death. Steve, his mother, Tricia, has requested that you speak at his funeral, if you're willing."

Pressure built inside him. He knew it was the right thing to do, but to be the focus, even if only for a few minutes, at a funeral brought him back in time to when his family died. The funeral guests had all clustered around and fawned over him. They kept talking about poor Steve, alone with his family gone. His neighbors and his dad's older sister had made such a fuss over him.

Yet when the services were over and the lawyer asked his aunt to take guardianship over her nephew, she'd flat out refused. It seemed her affection for him only lasted long enough to find out if there would be any sort of inheritance coming her way. When there wasn't, she washed her hands of him and walked out.

No one else had wanted the bother of a teenage boy either. Not even one that was a straight A honor student.

Which was how he ended up in the system.

A discreet hand brushed his. His head popped up. Joss removed her hand, but the chief's compassionate gaze stayed on him. The chief knew about his past. He'd understand if Steve declined Tricia's request. Oddly, this knowledge made him stiffen his spine. He would not let Tricia down. His colleagues in the Sutter Springs Police Department were more than coworkers. They were family. He would honor his fallen brother the best he could.

"Please let her know I'll do it."

The chief nodded, approval radiating from his face.

They moved on to other points of interest. The chief whistled silently when Steve told him about their conversation with Emily. Joss flinched when the woman's name was mentioned. He guessed she'd always be "Linda" to Joss.

"The clothes and doll will need to be entered into evidence."

"About that, sir." Steve glanced quickly at Joss before facing the chief again. "Chief, I'd like to hang on to the items. If we find Joss's family, they might need to see them to preliminarily prove her identity before any DNA tests are run. I'd also like to take Emily's phone out of evidence. She said we needed her journal to catch Kevin and find Joss's birth family and mentioned the phone would have what we needed to find it."

"I see." The chief swiveled his chair toward the window for a moment. Steve waited him out. After nearly a minute, the chair rotated slowly around again. "I will allow this, Sergeant. Finding Kevin is our goal. And if we can end the suffering of a family at the same time, that's even better. I'll let Officer McCoy know you're on your way to claim the phone. If there's anything else you need, ask. This case is high priority."

Steve nodded. "We'll need to start a search of crime records for unsolved kidnappings and missing persons, but we don't know which state to focus on."

"Use whatever personnel you need, Sergeant."

"Yes, sir." Steve took it as a dismissal and stood. Joss followed suit.

Within five minutes, he and Joss were standing outside the evidence department, and he was filling out the form that would allow him to remove the phone from evidence. Steve finished the form and handed it to Officer McCoy with a flourish. She shook her head at his antics.

"I'll be right back." Officer McCoy took the form and disappeared. Joss's phone rang.

"It's the hospital," she told him, showing him the display. "I'll go over there."

"Don't go too far."

She rolled her eyes. "I'll stay in view."

Officer McCoy returned a minute later with the phone, sealed in an evidence bag. Steve took the device and pocketed it. He glanced over at Joss. Her back was to him, but he could tell she was still on the phone. He turned back to his colleague. They talked about the case for a few minutes, giving Joss privacy. Both officers jumped when Joss cried out behind them.

Whirling, Steve's gaze shot to Joss. She stood braced against the wall, arms crossed over her stomach and bent over, her face contorted as if she were in pain. Her cell phone lay on the ground where she'd dropped it.

"Joss!" Rushing over, Steve took her in his arms, not caring who saw him. McCoy was right behind him.

She picked up the phone and spoke into it. Steve edged her away from the officer.

"Joss. Honey, what's wrong? Are you hurt?"

"Steve," Officer McCoy said. He looked at her. "That was the hospital. They called to report that Linda Graham is dead. She's been murdered."

NINE

"Murdered," Steve wheezed, the breath knocked out of him. "We were there less than two hours ago. How—what happened? We had a guard posted."

Joss sobbed into his shoulder. He winced, wishing he had the option to wait and ask for details later. But he didn't. He was a cop and a victim had died on his watch.

"Joss, why don't you go wait—"

"No!" She thrust him away from her. Tears streamed down her cheeks. She wiped them away and visibly pulled herself together. "That woman, she was my mother, she raised me for over twenty years. I need to know how this could happen."

"Let me get all the details and I will find you," Officer McCoy said.

Steve agreed quietly, then led Joss back to the chief's office. When they walked in, the chief raised his head then jumped to his feet. Striding around the desk, he approached them.

Keeping his voice low, Steve gave him the gist of the latest development. The chief's eyes widened with each word. Soon, Joss was seated, the chief on her left and Steve on her right. She gave no sign that she was aware of either of them. Her tears had stopped, and now she sat, stunned.

Steve was worried. He'd heard of people going into shock upon hearing traumatic news.

Both Steve and Chief Spencer stood when Officer McCoy entered the room. She walked past both men and handed Joss a large ceramic mug. Chocolate-scented steam rose from it. Joss shuddered. When she took a small sip, Steve's shoulders drooped.

"Thanks, Officer McCoy," Joss murmured in a hollow voice.

"Melissa," the officer corrected.

"Melissa." Joss's lips trembled as she lifted them in a small smile.

Steve cleared his throat. He didn't want to be indelicate, but, including the decoy shooter, Emily was the fourth person to die in less than three days. He needed to know how someone had gotten beyond the safety measures they'd put in place. It was urgent.

"Right." Melissa McCoy moved in front of the group, standing with her hands clasped behind her back, and delivered her report. "Sir. The officer on guard reported that his water bottle had been contaminated. Some sort of sedative had been dropped in it. When he was out, the perp snuck into the room and smothered the victim."

Joss squeaked. Melissa flushed. "Sorry, Joss."

"Keep going," Joss choked out in her distress.

"The cameras caught the man going in and out of the hospital. He was most likely disguised, but they sent us the images. Chief, check your email."

Chief Spencer rose and moved behind his desk. With a few taps on his keyboard, he brought up his email and downloaded the images in question.

"Joss, do you recognize this man?"

She looked at the images. She started to shake her head, then froze. Steve saw recognition flash across her face. She leaned in, her nose inches from the screen. "That's him. His hair and beard are different, but those are his eyes. And look." She pointed to his face. "See that scar, it's barely noticeable. I didn't even realize it was there the first time I saw him. It didn't register. But now, I remember seeing it when he shot at us before."

She meant she saw it when she was staring down the barrel of his gun. Steve flexed his fingers. Drawing in several deep, slow breaths, he tried to calm himself. He needed to keep a rational perspective. If the chief believed Steve would lose his cool or in any way jeopardize the successful completion of the case, he'd assign him to desk duty, regardless of how short-staffed they were.

Steve straightened his fingers and forced his stiff shoulders to relax. Joss was safe. She was here, and he would keep her safe.

"I need to find my mom's journal." Joss spoke suddenly, emphasizing the word *mom*. He wasn't sure if it was for her benefit or theirs.

"Where do you think she might have hidden it?" Chief Spencer edged away from her.

When she relaxed at the increased distance, Steve imitated his superior's movements. To his surprise, her hand shot out and grabbed his arm. All right, then. He'd remain where he was. He preferred staying near her, anyway.

Which wasn't a good sign.

He ignored the warning bells clanging internally. It wasn't about him. At the moment, Joss was all that mattered. And finding justice for

Emily, Tim and Hal. They'd all died for whatever was in that journal.

"I won't know until I search through her phone." Her head shot up, and her gaze swung from person to person. "I have to plan a funeral."

Whatever composure she clung to dissipated. Joss collapsed on her chair and covered her face, her body shaking with silent sobs.

That did it. Regardless of whether or not anyone saw or judged him, Steve drew a chair closer until it butted against hers. Sitting down, he gathered her into his arms.

"It's okay, Joss. We'll help you. You're not alone."

The distraught woman turned and tucked her face into his neck. His embrace tightened. He shifted so he could meet the chief's concerned gaze. The chief nodded.

"What now?" Steve mouthed.

"Joss." Melissa squatted down in front of him. "You can't stay on your own tonight. Nor can you go home. Not after all that's occurred. I have a spare room at my apartment, and the security's sound. Plus, it's only a few minutes from the station."

Steve bit off his protest. Melissa's suggestion had merit. He had been on almost constant guard for two days. He wasn't a robot. God didn't make humans to run continually without rest. He needed sleep if he wanted to function. "I know you need to take some time to look through your mom's phone. Maybe it would be easier to cope if you weren't surrounded by all her memories."

He grimaced. It sounded mushy to him, but he was trying to be sensitive. He recalled the total devastation when his parents and sisters were killed. Everywhere he went, he was reminded of the twins' smiles and the games they played. Or of his mom's love of music and nature.

Or the absolute fury in his soul at his father. He'd prayed to be able to forgive him, but his blood still pounded in his head when he considered the man.

He wiped his brow, then slid back from Joss, gently disentangling his arms from her slim back.

"Miss Graham—"

"Joss," she cut the chief off. "I can't—that name only reminds me of all the lies."

Steve ducked his head. He'd probably feel the same way.

"Fine. Joss, then," Chief Spencer said. "Go with Officer McCoy. In the morning, I will have officers at her home to assist you with whatever you need."

"Chief, what about extra security tonight?" Steve asked.

Melissa rolled her eyes at him. "Relax, hero. Nicole and Kathy are both off duty. We'll have a slumber party."

He snickered. "Are you sure Nicole will be up for it?"

Lieutenant Nicole Quinn had only been married for a year. She and her husband, an ex-FBI special agent, lived in the countryside with their adopted daughter, Chloe.

"Sure, she will. Jack can spare her for one night."

He raised his eyebrows but refrained from commenting further. Even if only Kathy was on protective detail, that would place two skilled cops on the premises within reach. Plus, as she'd mentioned, the place was secure.

He yawned. As much as he hated to admit it, he needed to be home in his own bed. She'd be safe, he told himself. It was only one night.

What could happen?

Joss didn't want to be separated from Steve, but if she protested, she'd appear needy. So she kept her gaze down and went along with the rest of the group. Who was she to question the experts? Her brain was mush inside her skull.

If she leaned over, it might leak out her ear. She desperately needed a distraction.

A slumber party with a group of Sutter Springs police officers didn't sound like her idea of fun, but it was the best offer she had.

She didn't want to leave Steve.

Her spine tautened. Oh, no. She refused to become dependent on a man. She'd done fine her whole life and enjoyed her independence. Joss had a job she enjoyed, a lovely home.

An empty home. And acquaintances instead of friends. Unconsciously guided by her itinerant past, she'd built a hedge around herself, remaining isolated rather than making friends she'd be asked to abandon.

Now, she was all alone.

That was why she wanted Steve to stay. Not because she had developed feelings for the handsome sergeant, but because she was comfortable in his presence and didn't want to be by herself.

Deliberately, she stood and sauntered away from him. Her side grew cold now that he wasn't next to her. She ignored the fanciful sensation. Glancing his way, she met his gaze, then averted hers, uncomfortable with the puzzled frown carved on his features.

"I'll start diving into the missing persons database," he announced. "See if there were any abducted female toddlers in Amish communities twenty-two years ago."

Maybe he wasn't upset after all if he could carry on business as usual.

"You'd have to cast a wide net, Sergeant. I'd say it would be better to narrow down the Amish communities we are targeting."

Sighing, Steve ran a hand through his short hair, making it stand up in places. Exhaustion melted onto each feature. His posture, too, seemed weighed down, as if he had a heavy burden on his back. Even if he wasn't physically tired, recent events would leave anyone emotionally drained.

Pity twisted her heart. And guilt. She'd been so wrapped up in herself, she hadn't thought about all he'd done for her. She wasn't the only one who'd lost someone today.

She padded over to him, placing a hand on his arm.

Startled, his head reared back.

"Maybe that task can wait?" she whispered. "You're done in. A few more hours can't hurt. Tomorrow morning, we can tackle it, and search for the journal. Yes?"

Cautiously, he placed a hand on hers and squeezed. Then he dropped his arms and pivoted away from her. "I guess Joss is right, Chief. I'm so tired, I'm not thinking clearly."

The chief strolled to the door and pushed it open. "I think that's wise. Joss, I'll leave you in Officer McCoy's care. Officer McCoy, keep me informed of your location at all times. I can get someone else to start the preliminary search for missing Amish children in the appropriate time period."

"Yes, Chief."

"Sergeant Beck. Go home. Get some rest. But be back on duty at eight tomorrow morning. The sooner we catch this perp, the better."

Dismissed, Joss walked out of the police station, sandwiched between the two cops. Both of them began scanning the surrounding area the instant they stepped outside. Another time, it might have been funny, and she would have made a comment laughing. Tonight, it was sad. Melissa waited until Joss was in the cruiser before she relaxed her guard and opened her own door.

Steve hovered near the car. Melissa rolled down the window. "Relax, Steve. I've got her. I sent Kathy and Nicole a text. I haven't heard from Nicole yet, but Kathy's getting a bag together and she'll meet us at my apartment."

Steve nodded and spun around. Joss stared

after him, wishing he'd stayed. Knowing why he hadn't. But still, it hurt when he didn't even glance back over his shoulder. As if she wasn't that important.

I'm a case to him. No doubt, when this Kevin person is found and put in jail, he'll move on to the next one and I'll go on with my life.

A life that she wouldn't recognize as hers anymore.

Enough. She wouldn't get maudlin. Steve was an honorable cop tracking a killer. That was the extent of their relationship. She shut out the tiny voice in her mind calling her a liar and threw herself into a conversation with Melissa. The pretty young officer was easy to talk with. If they'd met in another circumstance, they could have been friends.

If Joss had let her in.

Kathy met them in the parking lot of the apartment. She carried a fuchsia duffel bag over one shoulder. Joss blinked. Kathy didn't seem the fuchsia type.

"Hey." Kathy sauntered up to them as they exited the cruiser. She strategically placed herself on Joss's other side, sandwiching her in again. "Nicole's coming around eight. She's out with Chloe."

"Great! It'll be fun." Melissa took out a security pass and buzzed them in.

Fun. Joss shook her head. She was way too mentally wiped out to think of anything being fun. All she wanted was to sleep and forget this day had ever happened. She wanted to wake up and find that Linda was still alive and still her mother.

It wouldn't ever be the same. She needed to accept that.

The apartment was on the first floor. It opened into the living room area. The kitchen was small, really only big enough for one person to comfortably work. It opened into a dining area large enough for a decent-size table. A long hallway led back to the bathroom, a closet and two bedrooms. Melissa pointed out the twin beds in the room at the end of the hall.

"You and Kathy will sleep here. I'll be in the room next to you, and Nicole will use the sofabed in the living room."

Joss didn't argue. She knew Nicole was there to add an extra layer of protection for her.

Lieutenant Nicole Quinn arrived at eight fifteen. Joss's eyes widened at her first sight of the tall glamorous woman. She was a cop? Nicole Quinn was gorgeous, but the smile she beamed at Joss was sincere and lacking in conceit. She brought several containers of Chinese food with her.

"Good. I didn't want to cook." Melissa grabbed two of the boxes and ordered Kathy to round up plates and silverware. Kathy rolled her eyes but did as asked.

"I'm the lieutenant, Missy. You're the officer."

"Yeah, yeah. It's my place, so I make the rules and give the orders."

Amidst the banter, Joss sank back into the sofa cushions. Her mind felt muzzy. It was difficult to think clearly. Tomorrow, she knew she'd have to deal with reality.

Her back pocket buzzed. Frowning, she reached back and pulled out a phone. Her mother's phone. She'd nearly forgotten. Linda had told her the clues to finding the truth were on the phone. The woman had been heavily medicated, though. What would be on the device?

In her heart, she wasn't yet able to think of the other woman as Emily, although she knew that was her real name.

Well, she wouldn't find out tonight. The buzzing she'd felt was the phone shutting off.

"I think the battery is dead." She waggled the cell at the other three women. "I don't have a cord for this model."

"No problem." Melissa waved her hand toward the kitchen counter. "I have a cordless charger. Just set the phone on it."

Standing, Joss went to the charger and set the phone on it. Nothing happened. "Is this supposed to light up or something?"

Melissa rose and strode over. "It should turn blue around the edges. It's kind of sensitive. Maybe the case is too thick. Try taking the phone out of it."

Shrugging, Joss dug the device out by the top corner, separating the phone from the protective case. Something fell, pinging on the linoleum floor. Bending down, Joss picked up a tiny key that had been hidden inside the case.

"What is that for?" Kathy gestured to the key.

Instantly, the other cops surrounded Joss, sharp gazes focused on the small silver key.

"I have no idea. But I think this might lead me to the missing journal."

TEN

Steve had gone home and headed straight to bed. Not that it did him much good. He tossed and turned for an hour before slipping into a light doze. His dreams that night were full of the crash that had killed his family. His sisters were crying, his mother was screaming and his father demanded, "Why didn't you stop me?"

The dream shifted and Joss was in the car, instead. "Why didn't you save me?"

He jerked out of sleep and tossed aside the covers. It was only four thirteen, but he shook off the sleep-induced fog clinging to him. He would be better off getting an early start than surrendering to the nightmares again.

He hadn't had those dreams in a long time. For some reason, this case was messing him up. It was Hal and Tim. It was seeing an explosion a mere two feet from where he stood.

It was Joss.

He needed action. Striding to the kitchen, he glanced at his phone. And grimaced. He'd missed three texts. Two from Kathy and one from Melissa. Unlocking his phone, he read them and whistled. A key. Now, that was interesting. He glanced at the time. He couldn't go over yet. It wasn't even five in the morning. He could probably swing by at seven thirty. This was an urgent situation.

And what if they were still asleep?

He scoffed. Nicole, at least, would be up and about by then. If necessary, he'd wait in his car until they were ready. The important thing was to be there, able to hit the ground running, the moment they said the word.

He shot off a quick text to his colleagues. I saw your texts. I'll be there at seven thirty. Hitting Send, he grabbed a quick glass of milk and gulped it down before heading to the shower. By the time he was shaved and dressed, Melissa had responded.

We're all up. Should be ready by then.

Grabbing his keys off the hook on the kitchen wall, he bounced out the door and jogged to his cruiser. For the first time, excitement shuddered through him. The key had to be important or

Emily wouldn't have gone to the trouble of hiding it. It seemed significant that Joss didn't recognize it.

One more secret she'd been keeping.

Hopefully, today those secrets would begin to unravel.

Starting the ignition, he headed to Melissa's. Darkness shrouded the landscape. A few rays of red and yellow peeked over the horizon. By the time he arrived in the parking lot, the sun had risen, and bright beams lit every edge of the perimeter. Steve backed into a spot that provided a clear view of the front door. He sent another text letting the slumber party participants know he was there. He grinned, when he sent the text, knowing Kathy would grouse at the words *slumber party*. She'd tell him she was too old for such shenanigans, but Kathy was only thirty-four, just three years older than he was.

Movement in the bushes caught his attention. Turning his head, he narrowed his gaze and peered into the thick branches.

A man slouched down, his back pressed against the brick building.

Steve's hand drifted to his weapon. It was too late to try and sneak up on the suspect. The sunlight glinted off the man's wire-framed glasses an instant before his eyes met with

Steve's. They widened, then he sprang into action, leaping over the hedges and sprinting toward the back of the apartment complex.

Steve was out of his car and giving chase in less than two seconds, adrenaline pumping through his blood. Even with the head start, he was no match for Steve. Catching him before he rounded the corner, Steve jerked his hands behind his back.

"Who are you?"

The man struggled for a second, panting. The run had winded him. The faint odor of tobacco drifted from his coat.

"I haven't done anything wrong."

Steve gently pushed him forward, returning to his cruiser. "If you weren't doing anything wrong, why did you run when you saw me?"

The man hesitated. Probably trying to come up with a believable excuse. The front door of the complex banged open and he wilted. Steve turned as Joss and his colleagues greeted him at his cruiser. He tightened his grip, making sure his prisoner stayed caught.

"What do you have?" Nicole asked pleasantly.

"I saw him skulking around behind the bushes. He ran when he saw me. I'm still trying to ascertain what he wants."

"Me."

They all switched their focus to Joss. Her face was pale, but her jaw was set. Fury radiated off her skin. He imagined if he touched her, she'd be vibrating with the force of her anger.

"Joss, do you know this guy?"

She shook her head. "Not his name. But now that he's here, I realize I've been seeing him around the past couple of weeks or so. At the store. Outside the doctor's office."

She took a step closer until she stood toe-to-toe with the stranger. "Why have you been following me?"

"Yeah," Steve growled. "I'd like to know that, too."

Was this another man hired by Kevin? He was pretty sure if he'd been the man who'd shot at Joss and Emily, she'd have said so. Just how many people were involved in this travesty?

"My name's Calvin Wallace. I'm a reporter. I've been tracking Emily Hogan for two years in an attempt to find her husband, Kevin Hogan, and see he pays for the murder of my fiancée."

Joss could hardly believe her ears. But then, a thought struck her. "You left that note on the windshield, didn't you?"

Calvin sighed. "Yes. Not my brightest move. I was so frustrated. I thought if I scared her enough, she'd go and lead me to the evidence she'd gathered on Kevin."

Steve leaned forward. "How did you know she was hiding evidence?"

"My fiancée used to live next door to Emily. She was going by the name Shelley Grace then."

Joss shook. Another alias? How many had she assumed over the years?

"They'd gotten friendly," Calvin continued. "One day, when she dropped over to see Emily, she saw a book of some kind on the table. She hadn't meant to look, but when Emily freaked out, she knew it was serious. She convinced Emily to talk with me."

"Why not the police?" Steve asked.

"She told Brandi, my fiancée, that her husband had ties pretty high up. She wasn't sure who to trust. But if she gave me the evidence, I could research the husband and destroy him."

"Did she give it to you?" Joss burst out, holding her arms around herself.

He shook his head. "The next day, Brandi called me to say a man was following her. Then the call cut off. When they found her body, it was labeled a random mugging gone wrong. I

knew better. So did Emily. She called me, told
me she was sorry, she knew Kevin Hogan was
responsible, but she had a child to protect. Then
she disappeared again."

Me. I was the child.

Joss swayed, bumping into Kathy. The sturdy
lieutenant put her arm across her back, lending
her stability. Stiffening her spine, she straightened. She would not show any weakness.

Steve caught her glance, one eyebrow lifted.

"I believe him," she whispered.

He released Calvin, backing away and giving
the reporter space. Calvin rubbed his wrists,
grimacing.

"Yeah, I do, too."

"What now?"

Steve shrugged. Then he peered at the reporter. "Did your fiancée tell you anything at
all that might have been helpful?"

Calvin rubbed his jaw. "Well, it won't help
you catch Kevin Hogan, but you might be interested in this little tidbit." He pointed at Joss.
"While she didn't specifically say she was talking about you, she did mention that her husband had been paid a lot of money to find a
child for a wealthy family willing to overlook
the legal details."

Joss sucked in a deep breath. This was it. If

he knew this, maybe they could find out where she was actually from. Anxiety slid down her spine. Once they started down that road there was no looking back. But she had to know. And she owed it to the family who lost their child so long ago to let them know she was safe.

"Did she happen to mention where he found this child?" It felt odd referring to herself in the third person, as if she weren't standing right there completely aware of who they were talking about.

"She did. And I believe that there is a reason you have been in this area for so long. According to Emily, you were abducted less than an hour from here."

"Less than an hour?" Steve interrupted. "That narrows down our search considerably. Joss, we need to get back to the station. I want to start sending out inquiries to the police stations within an hour from here with Amish communities nearby. And you need to start looking at your mom's phone and seeing if we can find out where she had that journal."

Calvin blinked at them, his jaw dropping. "So, you're not charging me with anything? I'm free to go?"

"You weren't actually breaking any laws," Melissa stated. "Besides, I'd say you've already suffered." She handed him a card. "Stay in the area and contact us if you think of anything else. And give us your address and phone."

Calvin started to rattle off the information fast, and Melissa jotted it down on the back of another card.

On an impulse, Joss reached out to him. "If Steve says it's okay, I'll let you know if we get him."

"We?" Steve murmured, shooting her a side glance.

"You know what I mean."

"I do. I can't promise it'll be much, but we'll let you know anything we can."

"Sounds good. I promise not to print anything without your go-ahead."

Steve opened his mouth to say something but stopped when Joss moved to his side. Instead, he said, "I'm taking Joss to the station. Melissa, can you finish here? Get all the information regarding Brandi's death."

"Can do. We'll talk later."

Five minutes later, Joss was snuggled into Steve's car as the familiar scenery rushed past her window. "It's funny. I've driven on this road for so long. And suddenly it all seems strange to me. Why do you think she moved us so close to where I was taken?"

She couldn't bring herself to say the name Emily, but to call her Linda now just seemed wrong. It was all a lie. But, judging by what Calvin had said, there was some hope that the woman who raised her had acted to protect her and not in her own self-interest.

Steve hugged the curve as they moved past the lake. "Honestly, Joss, my guess is that she was really hoping to be able to reunite you with your family but just never got up the courage to do it."

A couple hours later, Steve brought her a breakfast sandwich and coffee in the station's conference room. "I ordered out." They'd both faced disappointing news when they had arrived—the chief's order to search missing persons cases had not turned up anything specific yet, just a whole lot of hurt, stories of children gone from their families but nothing that matched her circumstances. Joss herself had worked on her mother's phone, looking for clues, but nothing had popped to give them direction.

Gratefully, she sank her teeth into the egg-and-cheese muffin before taking a sip of the piping hot coffee.

"Thank you. This hits the spot. How have

your inquiries gone?" Steve had been calling police departments in the area, working from his desk and periodically checking on her.

He avoided her gaze for a moment before sighing and taking the chair next to her. When his hand covered hers, she knew it was serious. "Honey, I talked with a buddy of mine. He's the chief at the police department the next town over. He searched his files and found a case that fits yours. An Amish child, youngest of five children, went missing on March 29th twenty-two years ago. She was never seen again."

She couldn't breathe.

"Joss!"

"I'm okay. Really." She aimed a wobbly smile at him. "It's just a shock to realize I truly was abducted. I'll be fine. So, is he notifying the family?"

Steve stared at her for a moment before sitting back in his chair. His hand slid from hers. "The oldest son is a friend of his. He was letting him know, and once he does that, we'll figure out how to proceed. Now, there is a possibility that it could be a coincidence, and we want to be careful not to get their hopes up."

She snorted. "Haven't we had the coincidence conversation before?"

"Just saying. So, how is your mission going?"

She held up her mom's cell phone. Emily's phone. "It's going. My mo—Emily took a lot of pictures of nothing."

"Anything in the notes?"

"Nope. She didn't even write a grocery list. She wasn't big on doing any writing on it. I think whatever we're looking for will be in the downloads or in the photos."

"Keep looking. I'm going to check my computer for anything that's popped up."

Two hours later, she sat up with a gasp as Steve returned from his desk in the station. "Steve!"

"What?"

"I've been going through the photos when I remembered the key. Look at this."

Pushing the phone across the table, she scrolled through the images. A street sign. The front view of a fitness center. A close up of the address. A locker. Followed by a picture of the locker number.

A locker with a tiny keyhole. Approximately the same size as the silver key burning a hole in her back pocket.

"Brilliant," he breathed. "It's at a public gym."

"We've never had a membership to a gym. At least, not that I can remember. Probably because we moved around too much." She smiled, hope bubbling inside her like a soda can that was shaken too hard. It was hard to contain. Her eyes fell again to the images on the phone. "It shouldn't be too hard to figure out which one. She's given us lots of visual information."

He scooted his chair over to a side table and snatched a laptop. When he rolled back to where she waited, he pulled up a map feature and began looking for nearby public fitness centers. Within fifteen minutes, they looked up at each other.

"That's it. That's the one." She switched her glance back and forth between the computer screen and the images on the phone.

"We'll head over—"

The conference room door opened. "Excuse me, Sergeant Beck. You have a visitor. A US Marshal."

The officer stood aside and ushered a tall man with sandy hair and intense blue eyes into the room. He was dressed in a suit and tie, and the shape of a gun was barely visible under his coat.

Steve stood. "Marshal?"

The visitor barely looked at Steve. His piercing stare remained on Joss, searching for something. "Marshal Micah Bender, Sergeant Beck. I'm here because twenty-two years ago, back when I was still Amish, my baby sister, Christina, disappeared."

Joss pushed herself to a standing position. Her legs shook. Her brother. This tall serious man was her brother.

ELEVEN

How could this be her brother? They didn't look anything alike. Joss peeked at Micah's profile from where she sat in the back of his SUV as they made their way to his parents' home. He and Steve were sitting in front, comparing notes.

That was her choice. She didn't want to sit up front because she needed a few minutes to process his entrance in her life and what it meant. Her stomach was tied in knots. They were less than twenty minutes out from where Edith and Nathan Bender resided. Her parents, she corrected herself. The names were those of complete strangers to her. Nothing about Micah, or anything he'd said about her parents and brothers, triggered any sense of familiarity.

Her hand tightened on the garment bag Steve had suggested she retrieve, just in case it would help prove or disprove her identity. Micah had smiled, a secretive half smile at the comment.

"You're my sister," he told her, no doubt in his dark voice. "I don't need to see any proof, and neither will our parents."

Our parents.

She couldn't understand how he was so sure. Although, an Amish child being reported missing was something of an anomaly.

A thought struck her. "Hey, Micah? How old am I?"

He tilted his head to see her in the rearview mirror. "Twenty-four. Your birthday was in August. The fifteenth."

She nodded. "That means I'm not much younger than I thought. You said we have brothers?"

Not until after she'd asked the question did it hit her that she accepted what he was telling her.

"We do. I'm the oldest. I recently turned thirty. Zeke's twenty-seven. Isaiah—" he hesitated "—Isaiah's next. He's twenty-six. We don't know where he is currently."

He sounded sad. Then she counted in her head. She blinked. So close together. "Wait. I thought there was another?"

He grinned at her. "Gideon. He'll be twenty-five on August fifteenth."

"I have a twin?"

Shouldn't she have had some kind of internal instinct about a twin? She laughed at the fanciful thought. Micah spun the wheel and turned into a driveway, pulling in front of a two-story white house. Behind the house, a red barn was situated between two fields. In one field, a couple of horses were grazing, heavy blankets on their backs to protect them from the weather. Inside the barn, a buggy was barely visible. Beyond the red barn, she could see a second barn.

She was born here. Shaking her head, she slipped out of the door Steve had opened for her. He brushed his hand down her arm as she walked past him. She appreciated the comforting gesture. He was here. She wasn't alone.

She was never alone.

God, I've not been very faithful lately. Help me through this.

They approached the bottom of the stairs. The door opened and an Amish woman exited the house, drying her hands on a dishcloth. Her brow furrowed as she watched her oldest son climb the steps. Micah leaned down and planted a kiss on his mother's cheek.

"Micah, I didn't know you were coming today." Her gaze fell on Joss standing at the bottom of the stairs. All the color left her face. "Nathan!"

Footsteps thundered inside the house. "Edith? What's wrong?"

An older, grayer version of Micah with a long beard burst through the door and out onto the small porch. Edith didn't say a word. She lifted one trembling hand and pointed at Joss.

Any doubts Joss harbored fell away. As much as Micah resembled their father, she was a younger carbon copy of Edith Bender.

"Christina," she breathed, stumbling down the steps toward her long-lost child. Her arms reached out and she grabbed Joss, gently holding her close. "My child. I have prayed for this moment for two decades."

Joss huddled in her mother's embrace, patting her back awkwardly. She didn't know this woman, but she couldn't back away from her mother.

"*Cumme*, Edith. Let them in out of the cold." Nathan brushed a tear from his cheek and held the door open, gesturing for their guests to enter the house. Joss started moving, then halted, peering over her shoulder at Steve. He jogged up the steps, his arm brushing hers as he came to a sudden stop next to her.

"All right?" His voice, pitched low, made her shiver. It was the situation. She was completely out of her depths and floundering. These feelings she had for Steve had developed so rapidly, there was no way they could be genuine.

The small group moved into the house. Edith pressed Joss into a wooden chair at the table. Steve sat on her left and Micah lowered himself into a chair across from her. Edith bustled around the kitchen for a minute, gathering plates, cloth napkins and a dish piled high with cinnamon rolls. Nathan fetched a coffeepot from the stove and several sturdy mugs before joining them, sitting at the end of the table. Edith placed the sweet smelling delicacies on the table before taking her own seat at the other end. A comfortable blaze in a wood burning stove heated the room.

She soon went from toasty to overheated and removed her coat, letting it fall behind her.

For a few awkward moments, no one talked. Her parents seemed content to stare at her. Squirming in her chair, she accepted a cinnamon roll from Micah. The moment she bit into it, she rolled her eyes as the delicate flavors hit her tongue.

"Christina." Edith frowned when she grimaced. "Is something wrong?"

Joss felt awful. "I'm sorry. I'm not used to responding to Christina. I've been called Josslyn, or Joss, for as long as I can remember."

Instead of appearing upset, her mother nodded. "Then we will need to learn to call you Joss. We might slip a few times. You've always been Christina to us."

Micah grunted. "I've tried to think about you as little as possible."

She reared back slightly. He shrugged.

"It was my fault you were taken."

"*Sohn.*" Nathan spoke in a slow, unhurried manner. "You were eight. You were not to blame."

"*Mam* asked me to watch my sister while she took care of Gideon." He turned to Joss. "He'd fallen and cut himself bad."

She nodded at him to continue.

"Isaiah and I were goofing off. When I looked up, you were gone. We weren't worried, not at first. You were an adventurous kid, always wandering off. But we never found you."

Her heart wrenched in her chest. To bear that burden as a child. "Is that why you became a marshal?"

"Mostly."

She could see he didn't want to talk about it, so she bit back her curiosity and allowed her parents to change the subject.

"Joss, why don't you show our parents the bag you brought?"

She made to stand, but Steve beat her to it. "You stay here. I'll get it."

When he left, the side where he'd been sitting seemed to grow cold. He returned within a minute and handed her the bag.

The moment she set the doll on the table, Edith covered her mouth. Her eyes glinted with unshed tears. "I made you that doll. I didn't need it, but if I did need proof that you are my daughter, that doll is it."

When the meal ended, Nathan stood, announcing he needed to check on the livestock. Edith began to clear the table. Steve caught Joss's hand when she made to help her mother. "Look. I need to continue the investigation. I should have followed your brother out here so I could head back. I suppose I could have another officer meet me here…"

That wouldn't go over well. They didn't have time for that. Joss's expression was oddly relieved. "We should go. The investigation has to take priority."

He smiled at her eagerness. He knew she wasn't comfortable. "I don't want to take you from your family."

She pressed her lips together. "My family is here, they know I'm alive and well, and we have time. I'm more concerned with finding Kevin and ending this. No one can have closure while he's walking around."

He had to agree with that. Tim's death, especially, was an open wound. He imagined Emily's was the same to her. They'd never be able to move forward until the villain of the story was behind bars. Joss would be in danger until that happened.

"I wonder if he thinks you already have the journal?" he mused.

"Maybe. After what Calvin said, I think we have to assume such a book exists. I'm sure the fact that I've lived with Emily for all these years makes me a liability. He has no way of knowing what I know."

Steve had been thinking along the same lines. "I agree. We must keep moving."

"Then I'm coming with you." Micah had been leaning against the wall. He pushed himself away and closed the gap between them. "Since we're here in my vehicle, it makes more sense than asking someone else to meet us here."

Steve didn't protest. Micah had as much a right as anyone else to help find the perp who stole his sister and ripped his family apart. He'd caught some of the nuances at the table. Micah carried baggage from the abduction. He wouldn't ask, but it sounded as though Isaiah did, as well.

"I'd be glad to have you. We need to check out a certain fitness center. I think from the map it's about twenty minutes from here, between your parents' house and Sutter Springs."

Micah rubbed his jaw. "What are we looking for?"

"My mother—the woman who raised me— she kept a journal. I think there's evidence in it that will incriminate the man who kidnapped me."

Micah's lips thinned at the mention of Emily. "That woman was not your mother."

He ground out each word.

Joss bit her lip. "I know. But, Micah, until a few days ago, I had no reason to suspect otherwise."

Micah sneered slightly, but then his expression softened when it landed on her distressed face. "Look, I'm glad you're back, that's all. You left a hole in our lives."

She nodded, still disturbed. As soon as Nathan returned from the barn, she broke the news that she was leaving with Steve to her parents.

Edith cried a little when she heard they were leaving, but Joss hugged her. "I'll be back. Honestly. I need to help Steve, though."

Which was how, ten minutes later, they were back in the vehicle, heading to the fitness center. "Do you have the key on you?"

"Of course." She patted her pocket. "I wouldn't leave something that important behind."

Micah kept up a steady hum of conversation with Joss as they drove along the picturesque roads. It could have been out of a painting, Steve mused as they passed a large farm with cows and three silos. Soon, they entered the business district and farms were replaced with stores and restaurants. A couple miles into town, Joss pointed suddenly. The gym from her mother's pictures loomed on the right.

"We sure picked a busy time to make this trip." Micah switched off the engine.

He was right. They'd had to drive around to find an empty parking space. The sidewalk teemed with people walking from one business to another.

"It has to be done. Stick close," Steve said. Micah dropped a quarter in the parking meter.

Steve started walking. Joss's shorter legs made it a challenge for her to keep up with the pace. Without thinking, Steve stretched out his hand and caught hers.

"To make sure we don't get separated," he explained.

Micah snorted. Heat climbed Steve's neck. He had a feeling Joss's newfound sibling was planning to have a brotherly chat with him later. Catching the other man glaring at him, he made a face. Yep. Micah would definitely be asking him about his relationship with Joss at some point.

He hadn't known her long, but he'd grown to admire her. She was strong and compassionate. And brave. If he were ever to find the perfect woman to grow old with… He couldn't go there.

Despite the attraction he felt for her, he didn't have a relationship with Joss. The thought hurt. He hardened his jaw. She had been through enough in the past few days. She didn't need to get involved with someone as broken as he was. When this case was over, she'd move on, get to know her family and one day find a man worthy of her.

His future stretched out empty ahead of him.

A small hand squeezed his fingers. He glanced down and met her questioning glance. Shaking his head, he tried to smile at her. It was hard to smile on the outside, though, when you were facing a brutal truth internally.

Micah held the door open for them, and they entered the fitness center together.

"We need to find the locker room," Steve

murmured, tugging her over to a map of the building. Micah strolled behind them. "It shouldn't be too difficult. This isn't a huge gym. Only two floors."

"There." Joss jabbed the map with her index finger.

Steve couldn't help himself. He took her hand again and the trio scurried through the gym and up to the second floor. They were so close to getting some real answers, but he couldn't shake the feeling that something wasn't right. Half turning, he walked backward a few steps, scanning the people meandering through the gym. None of them seemed to be paying any particular attention to them.

"I think the locker room should be down the next hall." Steve pointed to the corridor ahead to the right.

"You guys will have to wait here," Joss commented.

Micah frowned at her. "I don't want to send you off on your own."

"You don't have a choice." She lowered her voice. "According to the pictures, the locker is in the women's locker room."

Steve didn't like it, but he nodded. There wasn't any getting around it.

They arrived at the room. Joss glanced

around furtively. She pulled the key out of her pocket and held it in her palm. Steve hid a grin. She was cute when she was serious. Her hand shook when she opened the door. She ducked inside the room. The door closed behind her, severing his view of her.

Steve tensed. One minute passed. Then two.

"Should we go in after her?" Micah asked, leaning against the wall opposite the door.

Two young women approached, eyeing them suspiciously. They entered the locker room, whispering.

"We wait," Steve decided.

Both men sprang away from the wall when Joss reappeared, hugging a generic plastic grocery store bag.

"I haven't opened it yet. There were others in the locker room."

Steve nodded. "We'll look once we're in the car."

Steve and Micah arranged themselves on either side of Joss as they made their way back to the vehicle. Once outside the gym, Steve placed a gentle hand on her elbow, keeping her close. He didn't relax until she was tucked inside the vehicle. He climbed in beside her.

Joss waited until they were all inside before she relinquished her tight hold on the bag and set it on her lap and opened it. She reached in and pulled out a worn composition book.

Her mother's journal.

She began to flip through the pages. He read over her shoulder. When she came to a picture of a man with cold eyes and a sarcastic grin, she scooted nearer to Steve.

He peered closer. Kevin's name was written across the bottom of the page. "She wanted to be sure the police had an image."

Joss nodded, her lips trembling. Steve hunkered down next to her and wrapped her up tight in his arms. "I've got you."

He couldn't think of anything more comforting to say. She sniffed and leaned into his arms for a second or two, then pulled away. Flipping another page, she gasped. "That's me!"

She'd been a beautiful child. Emily had kept track of the date and place she'd found her. He took the journal and read out loud. "'Kevin kidnapped you and planned to deliver you to his client. I overheard him talking on the phone about it. He'd said even if they caught him, he had friends who'd get him out. Charges would never stick.'"

He ran his finger down the page. "She wasn't sure what they'd been talking about. Had thought he'd had a mistress."

Joss sobbed, her gaze running ahead of his. "Steve, he had me locked in his trunk."

Steve read further.

"She writes that was when she ran. She'd snuck into his office and taken a couple of papers from his desk. She wasn't sure what they were, but they looked important. Then she'd snuck off with you. And look here." He jabbed a paragraph lower on the page with his index finger. "Here she detailed what she knew of Brandi's murder."

"Look at this," Joss said. "She detailed every place we lived. She moved us often, to stay ahead of him. But look—when we were in Virginia, she was at the mall and saw an old acquaintance from a distance. One of Kevin's cronies. I remember that. I didn't understand why, but she pulled me out of school and the car was already packed. I was in third grade." She frowned. "I'd forgotten, but she changed our last name then. I was little, so I didn't question it too much, but I think we probably had several names during the years."

Steve paged through the journal. "You did. She has a list of your aliases here."

"I don't want to lose all this information." Snatching out her phone, Joss snapped pictures of a few of the more salient pages.

When she slipped her phone back into her pocket, Steve closed the journal and handed it to her. "Let's head back to the station. I want to get this information disbursed, especially Kevin's picture. We need to have the other departments looking out for him, too." Joss tucked the journal into the plastic bag.

He couldn't explain why he was feeling antsy, but his nerves were screaming that they needed to move out. "Let's get out of here."

Micah dipped his head in acknowledgement then turned around. Once the car was in motion, Steve relaxed against the seat.

A short while later, Micah pulled into the police station and let the other two out of the car. "I have to go, but I'll be in touch."

His eyes warned Steve that they were still going to have that conversation.

Steve waved him away. He visually scoured the parking lot. Nothing seemed suspicious or out of place, but he remained uneasy. Joss was a target as long as she was out in the open.

He hurried her into the station. Until she was safe, he wouldn't let down his guard.

The next two days were fraught with high emotions. Steve sent out the information he'd collected from the journal, but no news had come back. Joss and the Benders had DNA tests done and were awaiting results. The police department and the Sutter Springs community attended a series of funerals.

First had been the one for Emily, Joss's adopted mother. A private affair only attended by a few people—just Joss, some of her coworkers and him—it was a short but lovely service. Joss was careful to memorialize Emily as a good mother to her, emphasizing her finer qualities. He was filled with admiration for her strength and grace under terrible circumstances and her lack of bitterness.

Now they were dealing with Hal's and Tim's funerals.

"What happened to Princess?" Joss murmured as she stood beside Steve amidst the mourners. Her black dress emphasized how pale and drawn she'd become in the past few days.

"Hal's brother decided to keep her. She has a good home."

"I'm glad."

"Steve!" He turned to greet one of the troopers from the state police. Ben and Steve had attended the police academy together. They'd both started as shy cadets who'd grown into confident law enforcement officers. They spent a few minutes catching up and reminiscing about Tim. Looking at his watch, Steve blinked. They had been talking for seven minutes. He made his excuses and turned back to apologize to Joss.

Except she was no longer at his side. Tension seized his muscles. Maybe she decided to give him space and wandered about the funeral home. He stalked from the room, scanning the mourners for any sign of her dark ponytail waving in the crowd.

She wasn't in the hall. He strode to the cloak room. When he still couldn't find her, he had one of the women officers check the restroom for her, tapping his fist against his thigh as he waited. When she emerged shaking her head, his heart dropped.

Joss wasn't in the funeral home. He ran to the coatrack. Her coat was still hanging up. She hated being cold. He'd seen the way she stood close to the heater vents or how she dressed in warm layers. She would not go outside without her coat, not when the windchill was nineteen.

Not by choice.

TWELVE

Joss shivered, staring into the cold eyes of the hired killer who'd shot Linda Graham five days earlier. A lifetime had passed in that handful of days. Was it all to end now, while the entire police force was inside honoring a fallen cop?

"You've given me more grief than you're worth," the man snarled.

His voice is higher than I thought it would be, Joss thought irreverently. She searched around for a way out, but he held her arm in a vise grip, and she couldn't yank herself free. He thrust her out the back door. The frigid wind whipped through her. She was going to die and all she could think was she'd left her coat inside.

He shoved her further out into the cold, the nozzle of his gun digging into her side. "We'll go someplace quiet to finish this conversation."

Joss stumbled on the uneven pavement but managed to remain upright. Each step they took separated her further from safety, from Steve. The man was bold, she'd give him that. To steal her out from under the noses of all those cops. Bold, or desperate.

"Why are you doing this?" She grunted when he pushed the gun deeper.

"It's nothing personal. I have a contract to fulfill, and I don't get paid until it's complete. I'm only half done. That does me no good."

Half done. Emily was the first half. She was the second.

"Why does someone want me dead?" She knew why, of course, but maybe talking would distract the hitman. Give her an opportunity to run.

"Stop talking," he spat. "I don't need to know, and it wouldn't do you any good to know."

An engine hummed ahead of them. Hopeful, she glanced up, praying for someone who could assist. The breath stuttered in her chest. The car she'd seen the night Emily was shot was parked a few feet ahead of them, running. Joss dug in her heels. He laughed and pushed harder. She was only five steps from her death.

"Police! Stop where you are and let the woman go."

Steve. She closed her eyes and slumped in relief. Her eyes bulged when a muscled arm caught her across the throat and swung her around. The gun remained pressed against her side. The hitman's breath stirred her hair as he held her in front of him like a shield.

"You shoot me, she dies, too. Face it, cop. This is a no-win situation," the hitman taunted Steve, inching toward his car and dragging Joss with him.

"You don't want to do this," Steve shouted.

"I do. I have no other option."

What other bargaining tool did Steve have?

The gun left her side. Her relief was short-lived as it tapped her temple. "She's dead, no matter how this all turns out. Either I kill her now or later, but she doesn't walk away."

"She walks away, but you don't," Micah countered, coming up from behind them. Joss couldn't see her brother, but she could tell he was close. "Put the gun down, and we'll talk. Work out a deal."

"No!" A shade of panic entered the hired killer's voice. "No deal!"

The gun was shoved against her temple again. The gunman half whirled her so she could see Micah standing beyond the running vehicle, his weapon fixed upon them. The pressure against her head increased. She flinched. He literally ground the point into her skin.

Crack!

The arm holding her prisoner jerked and went slack. She was free. Joss whirled around in time to see the hitman collapse back against the car, his vacant gaze aimed at the cloudy sky.

Steve replaced his weapon into his holster and strode to her. Joss fell against him, shaking. When his arms enveloped her, she snuggled closer, inhaling his familiar scent. She was alive. He'd shot the hitman, and she was alive. Unharmed.

Micah trotted up to them. "Joss? Did he hurt you?"

She shook her head, her cheek rubbing against Steve's chest. "No. He was hired to kill me and my—Emily. He said he wouldn't get paid until he finished the job."

Steve smoothed a hand down her ponytail. "He can't hurt you now."

Micah looked over at Steve. "That was some shot. Risky."

Steve shook his head. "I saw a chance and took it. Not taking it was riskier."

Reluctantly, Joss disengaged herself from his embrace. His arms fell away, but he stayed close. "Kevin's not going to stop coming after me, is he? He'll hire someone else. How will I even know if it's a bad guy walking toward me?"

Steve reached out and brushed a hand down her cheek, wiping away a tear. She hadn't noticed she was crying. "Do you trust me, Joss?"

"Yes, of course I do." Her list of trustworthy people was short, but Steve was ranked number one on it.

"Then trust that what I'm going to suggest is to protect you." He heaved a sigh and glanced between Joss and Micah. "Joss has a good point. I am going to have to deal with this—" He pointed at the body on the road. "You know there's always a brief inquiry when a fatal shot is fired. I might not have my weapon for a day or so."

"You won't be able to protect my sister." Micah nodded, his expression grim.

"Yeah. Not to mention we don't know who we'll be searching for. Micah, I know this is asking a lot, I know you're busy, but could you take her to your parents' house? Stay there with her until I get a handle on the situation here?"

Micah pondered for several long moments. "Yes. That might be the best plan. I know *Mam* and *Daed* won't mind."

Joss interrupted them. "Wait! I don't want to put my family in danger."

"Where's your faith, little sister? Since Emily never returned you, I think it's highly unlikely he'll look for you there." He being Kevin, she understood. Micah continued. "And I'll be there, too."

She didn't like it, but she wasn't going to make their job harder. These two brave men were rearranging their lives to keep her alive. "Okay. Will you take me home to pack a bag?"

This time, Micah shook his head. She scrunched up her forehead. Why wouldn't he let her pack?

"I don't think your house is a safe place right now," Steve informed her.

"And," Micah drawled, "you'll stick out like a peacock in a room full of doves dressed like you are. You're going to have to go undercover."

"Wouldn't that be lying?" She searched their faces. "I'm not Amish."

"Your family is. And you didn't leave us by choice." Micah held out a hand to Steve. "I'll see that my sister is safe. You take care of this dude out to get her so she can return to her life."

Steve shook his hand. "I will. Thanks for your help today. How did you know?"

Joss hadn't thought of that. Why was Micah there?

Micah smiled, a smile of such sweetness she caught her breath. Something about that smile touched her memory.

"I had to come. Your friend died saving my sister. It was my intention to honor his memory. When I saw you leave, I could tell you were searching for someone, and it had to be Joss. So, I searched, too."

He sketched them a wave and walked backward two steps. "My car is over there."

Facing forward, he left them alone.

Suddenly nervous, her teeth scraped her bottom lip. She turned her attention to the cop who'd just killed a man to save her life. She knew, looking in his face, he'd suffer for it. Taking a life was always serious.

"I don't want to send you away, but I have to, Joss."

"I get it. I don't want to interfere with your work or hinder what you have to do. And it will be good to spend a few days with my family." She didn't mention that the idea of spending an undisclosed amount of time with strangers whose way of life was completely alien to her gave her hives. What would be the point? Edith and Nathan Bender had been kind when she met them. And by now, they all had the expedited DNA results confirming they were her biological parents.

They've waited for my return for two de-

cades. I can be generous for a few days. And I am curious about them.

She raised her head, intent on making a light comment to diffuse the mood, but Steve's intense expression erased all thought from her mind. When his head drew closer, she didn't think—she reacted. Bouncing up on her toes, she latched her hands onto his arms and met his lips halfway.

The kiss started out as a barely there caress. He merely rubbed his lips against hers. When he leaned away from her, his gaze searching, she smiled. Happiness burst inside her like a sunbeam when he moved in for a second kiss.

Time ceased to exist for a few precious seconds. When Steve moved back, Joss blinked. Her arms fell to her side. Suddenly she shivered.

"You don't have a coat," Steve murmured.

"He didn't exactly give me a chance to grab it," she retorted.

The softness bled from his face. They both looked at the body behind them.

"I need to report this. You need to go." Despite his brisk tone, the hand reaching out for hers was gentle. "Let's get your coat, and then you can leave with Micah. I confess, I'll be able to focus when I know you're safe."

She nodded, her mood plummeting. On the way into the funeral home to retrieve her coat, he waved Kathy over. The tall lieutenant excused herself from her conversation and hurried to them.

"Kathy, there's a body outside. I need to take care of it. I'll explain later. Marshal Bender is waiting for Joss. Could you escort her to his car?"

Her heart fell. After that kiss, he was passing her off to another. Did he regret it? It was a mistake, she knew it. She didn't form attachments, but she'd forgotten for a moment. She thought, with Steve, she'd be willing to stretch herself and bend her boundaries a bit.

Except she couldn't get behind his boundaries. She knew his past had messed him up and he still suffered from it. There was nothing she could do about that.

When Kathy agreed, Joss silently got her coat and shrugged into it. She ducked her head to zip it, mostly to hide the emotions careening inside her. Steve walked over to her.

"I'm not abandoning you, Joss." Her head jerked up. He'd known what she thought. "I have to get this taken care of. When it is, I'll come and get you."

She searched his face. "Promise?"

It was rather bold of her to ask for a promise when she wasn't sure if she could keep such a promise herself.

He nodded. "I promise. Go with God, Joss. Keep me in your prayers."

"I will," she responded.

Always. No matter what.

It was the smile that had done him in.

Steve had been ready to apologize for kissing her, but then Joss had shot him a grin of pure sunshine. He had been kissing her again before his brain had a chance to kick in and tell him it wasn't a good idea.

He was on duty.

There was a dead man—that he himself had shot— mere feet from where they were standing.

He was supposed to be protecting her and finding Kevin Hogan. Getting romantically involved with Joss would destroy his focus. Obviously, it had already tampered with it. He sighed. Watching the sadness overtake the joy that had been on her face had hit him like a fist in his solar plexus. It had nearly stolen his breath.

That's why he made a promise to her.

And he'd keep that promise. Steve never went

back on his word. But he was pretty sure one or both of them was going to wind up with a bruised heart. Or worse. Joss deserved a man who could devote himself to her. After losing so much, how would she deal with someone who might get killed in the line of duty?

Tim was the first friend he'd lost. Watching his family and fiancée cope with the aftermath wasn't pleasant.

He had to get through the next few days. If he could find Kevin, then he could bring her home. Which meant she'd be free.

Would he?

Steve shoved the unworthy thought aside. He'd made his choices when he became a cop. Joss was the one who mattered now.

Leaving the funeral home, he walked back to where the chief and his boss were conferring. The coroner had already declared the cause of death and removed the body.

"We called Micah Bender," Chief Spencer informed him. "He will be available to make his statement at our convenience. Same with Joss. I'm having someone go to the Bender house to take those instead of having them brought in to the station. Was that your plan?"

Steve nodded. "Joss is in danger. We have no idea who Kevin Hogan will pay next. I doubt he's the type to get his own hands dirty. So far, except for the kidnapping attempt, he hasn't made any moves himself. I don't want her around here until we find him and stop this."

"I think this case will be rather cut-and-dried. I recognize the man you shot."

Steve's eyebrows rose. "Oh? Who was he?"

"He's a hard-core gambler who has apparently taken to hiring himself out for dirty jobs to pay his debts. He had some ugly characters he owed."

"Which would explain why he would choose to die rather than be arrested."

"It would, unfortunately."

He had to get through the next few days. Get his gun back. Find Kevin Hogan. Bring Joss home.

Then walk away. If he could.

THIRTEEN

All the books were wrong.

Joss stood beside her mother at the kitchen counter, clutching her aching sides, their laughter still echoing in the open space. Flour was scattered, covering them and every surface in sight.

She'd always heard the Amish were somber and didn't approve of laughter. She and Edith had spent most of the morning doing just that. Well, Joss's atrocious baking skills were partly to blame.

She had spent two pleasant days getting to know the Bender family. Micah stayed with them. Although she sensed some tension between him and his parents, the affection between them was obvious. He'd grumbled about donning Amish clothing again, but she'd pointed out that he stood out like she did in his *Englisch* clothes.

"Blend in, Micah," she sang out. "You need to blend in."

He scowled at her but marched down the hall and asked his father for a set of plain clothing.

She couldn't blame him for the scowl. She never wore dresses or skirts unless it was a fancy occasion. Even though the pale rose dress was a lovely color, she felt vulnerable in it. Plus, it had no pockets. Joss always had pockets.

But the hair was the tricky part. Getting all her hair braided and pinned neatly beneath the prayer *kapp*, now that took some serious dexterity. She was a little surprised to find that she had a mirror in her room. She'd always heard that the Amish didn't use mirrors.

"Mirrors aren't the same as pictures," her father explained. "You won't find them anyplace except your room. Vanity is wrong. But to use a mirror does not create a graven image, so it is not against *Gott*'s law."

She nodded at his reference to the Ten Commandments. She understood that part.

"Joss," Edith panted, "I think you should set the table, ain't so?"

She snorted. "Yeah. I can't mess that up, now can I?"

She grinned at the snicker that escaped from her mother's lips. "I think it will take more practice. Soon, my daughter, soon you'll bake like I do."

Joss rolled her eyes and turned to set the table.

The word *daughter* had snuffed out her laughter. She was torn between her loyalty to Emily, who'd done her best to protect her and had died for it, and this kind woman who had mourned her for so many years.

She had finished setting the table and was pouring out the water when the back door opened and the men of the family, except for Micah, tromped in. Gideon, her twin, shook off his boots, hung up his hat, then bounded over to give her a huge hug. It was the same way he greeted her every evening.

She found it endearing.

Zeke moved slower. He took off his own boots then straightened Gideon's, flashing a reproving glance at his sibling. When he had hung up his own hat and coat, he strode in, exuding quiet confidence.

"Joss," he greeted her.

She smiled at him. Zeke was taking his time to warm up to her, and that was fine. This large boisterous family overwhelmed her when they were all together.

Micah stomped down the stairs. "I heard the

buggy pull in. And I heard this guy—" he tousled Gideon's hair "—clomping around like a herd of elephants."

Gideon laughed and dodged away, plopping into his seat at the table. The rest of the men followed suit. Joss helped her mother carry the food over. She peered out the window as she gathered the freshly baked bread and the platter of butter.

It would be dark soon. Nathan was already lighting the kerosene lanterns in the kitchen. She was fascinated by the setup. Instead of lights in every room, the family had a sort of trolley cart with lamps on it. It was large and provided plenty of light. When they moved to the next room, the lantern cart would be rolled there. And if people were in both rooms, she'd seen the family lodge it next to the doorway, to light the downstairs. Having an open floor plan helped.

Would tonight be the night Steve came for her?

There had been no word since she'd been here. She ached to hear his voice. She wanted to know how the investigation was going, she told herself. In her soul, she knew she was lying. She missed Steve, his steady presence.

Bringing the bread to the table, she forced

her mind to focus on her family. They all lowered their heads to pray privately. Joss remembered Steve's request and said a little prayer for him, for his safety and his mission.

By the time the family headed to bed, her heart was heavy in her chest. He hadn't come. He hadn't texted to say he was well, or that things were progressing. She didn't send him a text either. What if a text could be traced? She'd heard of such things, although she'd never actually seen it happen. It was a risk she couldn't take.

Snuggling down in the bed, she said a silent prayer for Steve. Drifting off to sleep, her mind replayed that kiss.

Would he come tomorrow?

Steve slammed down the phone and grabbed his coat.

"What's your rush?" Kathy looked up from her desk.

"I have a lead on Kevin Hogan." He grinned at her, excitement drumming in his veins. "He got careless. He was overheard talking on his phone, hiring someone to kill Joss. He'd walked outside into the alley, unaware someone was listening."

"Do you need us?" Nicole sipped from her Pepsi can.

He considered it. "It might not be a bad idea for one of you to come."

Kathy and Nicole had been partners for years. They glanced at each other, and Kathy pointed to herself. When she got the go-ahead, she stood. "I'll come. She'll man the phones, just in case another call comes in."

"Once we catch him, the journal and this new witness's testimony should be enough to put him away for the rest of his life."

"Do we know where the call came from?" Kathy opened her door and slid into the passenger seat. "This might be a trap."

Steve shifted his car into Drive and pulled out of his spot. Approaching the road, he looked for oncoming cars before spinning his wheel and tapping the gas to increase the speed. He'd uploaded the address into his phone, which automatically connected to his car.

"I don't know who it was, so yes, it could be a trap. Which is how you might come in handy."

"Ah, I'm on-the-spot backup. Got it."

"My gut tells me this is legit. The voice sounded familiar." He shot her a quick glance. "He wouldn't give his name, but I think it was that Calvin guy. You know, the reporter?"

Her gaze widened. "Wow, really? He might be a bit of a loose cannon."

"Grief will do that to a person." He should know. He'd been living with that a long time. Her mouth worked, but she didn't say anything more.

The robotic voice of the GPS informed him to turn into the next driveway. It looked like an ordinary home. The walkway needed to be plowed. But nothing out of the ordinary. No warning bells went off.

Stepping from the car, he kept his hand on his gun as he started walking toward the house. He paused. His weren't the only fresh footsteps. The closer he walked, the more his hackles rose.

"Do you hear that?" Kathy whispered.

He did. Inside the house, two people were shouting. Maybe more, but he only heard two. He wasn't close enough to make out the words yet. Motioning for Kathy to move around to the back, he watched as she tossed him a thumbs-up before climbing over a snowdrift and slogging her way around the corner of the house.

He went to the front door. Raising his hand to knock, he changed his mind when a gun fired inside the house. Pulling his own weapon free, he crashed into the building, shouting, "Police! Drop your weapon!"

Kevin Hogan had a gun aimed directly at Calvin's chest.

Seeing Steve, Kevin pushed Calvin aside and dashed to the large picture window in the living room, raised his arms over his face, and threw himself through the glass. Sharp shards skittered over the floor, several streaked red with blood. Kathy burst into the house from the back door. She'd just missed him.

"Call 911!" Steve yelled, pointing at Calvin, leaning against the wall, his shoulder bleeding.

Calvin waved his hand weakly. "I got it. I got him on a recording. He admitted it."

The reporter passed out.

"I've got him, Steve. You go after Hogan." Kathy dropped down beside Calvin, her phone in her hand.

Steve didn't stick around. He ran outside and hopped in his car in time to see Kevin roar past in a sedan. Steve pulled out and slammed his foot on the gas while simultaneously hitting his lights and flipping his siren on. He jabbed the button to call dispatch.

"This is Sergeant Beck. I'm after the suspect and we are heading west on East Route 95. Lieutenant Bartlett is on the scene with the shooting victim and I am giving chase alone. I'm requesting backup to try and head off the suspect."

When he hung up from dispatch, Steve clenched both hands on the wheel and leaned forward. Kevin was driving rather erratically. It was possible he had been injured in the altercation with Calvin earlier.

Without warning, the sedan swerved and took off through a yard, bouncing over the snow-covered lawns. Making sure there were no people within view, Steve turned his wheel and followed. His teeth felt like they were going to rattle right out of his head, his car was bouncing so hard.

Kevin made another sharp turn, this time exiting the yards and careening on the next road. Steve called dispatch to inform them of the new direction.

He's heading for the lake, he thought, horrified. This no longer looked like a getaway. Kevin was making a suicide run.

"Come on, come on." His pedal was as close to the floor as it would go.

Ahead, sirens blared, and a cruiser cut off Kevin's escape route. For a moment, hope blazed in Steve. They'd stop him and he'd go to jail. His jaw dropped when the car sideswiped the cruiser blocking the way and continued driving.

The car crashed through the guardrail and

drove completely off the embankment. A moment later, there was a flash as Kevin's vehicle burst into flames. Steve ran up to the guardrail. Within seconds, the entire car was engulfed. He never saw Kevin Hogan emerge.

Hours later, the emergency crews picked through the scene. The coroner had taken the body for identification, and Calvin Wallace had been life-flighted to Cleveland. The recording he'd made had been entered into evidence.

Exhausted, Steve fell into bed that night. He didn't even bother to set his alarm. He only had one thing on his agenda for the next day.

Steve had a promise to keep.

FOURTEEN

The sun on his face jolted Steve awake. He threw out an arm and felt his way around the table next to his bed until his hand connected with his phone. Rubbing the sleep from his eyes, he checked the time. It was just after nine in the morning. He couldn't remember the last time he'd slept that late.

Swinging his legs over the edge of his bed, he yawned so wide, his jaw cracked. Time to get ready.

He took his time showering and eating his breakfast. This might be his last day with Joss. He knew he was procrastinating, putting off their final meeting when he'd have to tell her goodbye. But there were only so many things he could do to stall. Finally, he had no choice but to leave his house and hop in his cruiser to go fetch the woman who had captivated him, against his will and every instinct.

Would he have the strength to let her go once she was home?

His heart splintered thinking about it, but in the past few days, he'd realized, even though he could love her with his whole heart, he was also a cop, and that came with danger. He couldn't ask her, no matter how brave or spunky she'd proven herself to be, to settle into a life where pain and suffering was a possibility every day he left for work.

He'd enjoy this one last day.

It would have to be enough to last him a lifetime.

When he arrived at the Bender house, he'd barely left the car before a young Amish woman barreled from the house and threw her arms around him. Startled, he backed away.

The bonneted head tilted and his gaze met a familiar pair of brown eyes. He chuckled, shaking his head. "I forgot you'd be dressed Amish. I didn't recognize you at first."

She grinned, the happiness on her face messing with his pulse. "Come on in to the house. You can meet my brothers."

He looked at his watch. It was lunchtime. "I thought all the men would be at work."

"See that barn?" She pointed to the second barn behind the main one. "That's my dad's workshop. Convenient, right? That allows them to come home every day for lunch."

When she grabbed his hand to pull him along, he didn't have the heart to pull his away. He wanted her to be happy. Seeing her glow like this, it took his breath away. He tromped along beside her, up the stairs and into the house.

"Steve's here," she announced.

There was a second of silence before the chair legs scraped against the floor and he was surrounded by the Benders.

"You remember my parents, Edith and Nathan?" He exchanged greetings with them. "This is Zeke and my twin, Gideon."

Gideon had a face made for smiling, but he wasn't smiling now. His arms were folded across his chest, and a scowl was stamped on his face. It looked unnatural on him. "You've caught this man trying to hurt our Joss, *jah*?"

Steve decided he liked this young man. "He won't bother her anymore. He's dead."

The whole family gasped.

Joss tilted her head, frowning. "I am sad that someone died, but I am also immensely relieved that he won't be after me any longer. Is that awful?"

He touched her cheek. He couldn't help himself. "It's human. I felt the same way, although I was still horrified that he chose to kill himself."

He explained how the man had died.

She paled. "Steve, I'm so sorry."

Why was she sorry for him? Then it hit him. His family had died in such an accident. "Joss, don't worry about me. My family died a long time ago. I will always mourn them, but this was completely different."

She searched his face, checking to see if he was telling her the truth, before accepting his words.

"You must join us for lunch," Edith said. An invitation from Edith Bender was akin to an order. Before he'd had an opportunity to accept, he found himself hurried to the table and partaking in a hearty meal of beef stew, bread and homemade freezer jam. The brothers were all completely different. Micah, confident and brooding. Gideon, ebullient and bursting with enthusiasm. And Zeke, who took it all in and studied every angle before adding his two bits into the conversation.

Once lunch was done, Joss ran upstairs to change into her own clothes. Although she appeared happy to go, he was sensitive to her sadness at leaving her newfound family.

"You know where they live," Micah said. "And I'll be checking on you."

Joss rose up and kissed Micah's cheek. "Thanks, Micah. I mean it."

He flushed. "Listen, I have to be in Sutter Springs in two days. Why don't we plan on meeting for dinner?"

She nodded. "I'd love that."

Soon they were back on their way to Sutter Springs. "It'll be close to three when we arrive. You need anything in town before we go to your house?"

"No. I'm good. I'll wait to shop until tomorrow."

He peered at her. She was biting her lip again. It made her look so young. "Are you fine going back to your house? Do you want me to call Kathy or Melissa to come and stay with you?"

Her lips tilted in a quiet smile. "I am nervous. But it's my home. I can't let the memory of one man's evil steal it from me. I'll be fine. God will be with me."

The words sank into him. He'd said them before, but had he really trusted in them?

All too soon, they were entering Sutter Springs. *I need more time*, he wanted to yell. But his time was up. Nothing lasted forever. He had learned that lesson long ago.

At her house, he walked her to her door. He'd planned on leaving then, but he couldn't bear the thought of her entering a house by herself.

"Let me check. Just to be sure."

Walking ahead of her, he went from room to room, thoroughly looking in every crevice, inside each closet. When he returned to her, he gave her a tense smile and a thumbs-up.

"Thank you." She folded her arms across her body. "Now do you want to tell me what has you wound so tight?"

His time was up.

She'd felt the tension emanating from him from the moment they got into his cruiser to make the return trip. By the time they arrived, he was practically vibrating with it. Although she could see his concern for her in every glance, there was something else, too.

Even while her lips tingled with the memory of the kiss they'd shared several days earlier, her body shook with the sense of distance growing between them. He stood close enough for her to reach out and touch him, yet she couldn't make that connection they'd had earlier.

He was the cause. Something about him was keeping her out.

"I can't do this to you, Joss."

There it was. The beginning of her broken heart. "Can't do what, Steve? I haven't asked a single thing of you."

He hesitated. "I know. But I can feel us growing closer. It's no good."

She frowned, blinking the angry tears from her eyes. How dare he give up on them without giving her a chance. "Why are you saying this? Steve, what would be so awful about us trying to make a relationship work? Is it me? Is there something wrong with me?"

He flinched as her voice quavered. She tried to bring herself under control. "Joss, no!"

He touched her then, bringing her close and kissing her forehead. "You are amazing. You're beautiful, strong, smart, and you've kept faith even in awful circumstances. I'm the problem."

She snorted. Wasn't that always the excuse?

He tilted her chin to see her eyes. She read the torment on his face. "I'm a cop, Joss. I'll always be a cop. After this week, and what happened with Tim and Hal, you can't deny it's a dangerous line of work. Every day I clock in, I will face danger. And every evening, I might not make it home."

He broke from her and paced the room. "I look at you, and I want to ignore what my gut tells me. Then I think of Tim's family. I won't put anyone through that kind of fear."

When he faced her, a tear slid from her eyes. "I don't care. I don't. I had a lifetime with Emily as my mother. I miss her, but I don't regret her, even though she's gone. She's a part of me."

He wasn't buying it.

Frustrated, she clenched her fists and slammed them on her hips. "Who are you to tell me what risks I can take, Steve Beck? If I decide I love you, why is that wrong? God put you in my path that night. Not some other cop. He knew what He was doing."

He came closer and looked into her face. When he kissed her lightly on her lips, she thought they had a chance. Until she saw his face. He was saying goodbye.

Steve walked out the door. It banged behind him. She didn't go to watch him leave.

Two afternoons later, Micah walked in. Joss still hadn't come to terms with Steve's rejection, but she wasn't about to cry about him to her brother. After all, she'd known Steve longer than she had Micah.

They were talking awkwardly, when she burst out, "Micah, why aren't you married?"

His head reared back in shock. "That's quite a question, Joss."

"I know. But I'm trying to work something out in my head."

"Ah." He nodded, a half smile on his face. "Steve problems. I'll bet he's worried about his job and its effects on a relationship."

Her jaw dropped. "How did you know?"

A chuckle slipped from his lips. He leaned against the counter and loosely crossed his arms. "Because he's a man and he's in law enforcement. We all wonder, at some point, how our work will affect those we love. But this work, it's more than a job. Many of us feel it's a special calling. It isn't something I can walk away from, and I'm guessing neither can he."

She wilted in her chair. "So, it's a lost cause."

He snorted and strolled over to join her at the table. "No, it's not. It's just that some things need more time to work out. It might take him days, or weeks."

"Or never."

His expression sobered. "It is possible. My advice is don't give up on him just yet. Let him work his way through this."

"I can do that, if I have hope."

"Keep hoping." He pulled out his phone and

looked at the time. "If we want to hit a restaurant, we should leave soon."

Joss stood, then changed her mind. "You know what? I don't want to go out to eat. This is our first conversation alone, really alone. I want to spend the evening getting to know my brother without a bunch of people around."

He grinned. "I'm good with that. What do you propose?"

She sauntered to the refrigerator. "Well, our mom and I discovered I can't bake, but I can cook pretty decent. And with ice cream for dessert, we should be set." She opened the door and bent. The cold air brushed her face. "Hmm. Problem is, I have nothing to cook."

He stood. "I get the hint. Write me a shopping list, and I'll pick up whatever we need for a feast for two."

Taking him at his word, she scribbled down a list of ingredients. "Chocolate Peanut Butter Explosion? Is that a real flavor?"

"It is and it's the best ever invented." He grabbed his coat and left the house, running to his car. In a moment, she heard him drive away.

Humming, she danced around the kitchen, taking the clean dishes out of the dishwasher and returning them to their proper storage places. Micah's words tumbled through her head. There was still hope. She needed to give Steve time. She could do that. She could give him all the time he needed.

And if he still rejected her?

She stopped. If he turned away from her irrevocably, she'd have no choice but to move on with her life without him. She was getting quite skilled at moving past the bad and learning to adapt to the changes in her world.

Micah would be back soon. When he returned, they'd have dinner. Maybe she'd even ask him about Isaiah. She'd gotten the feeling that Isaiah was a prickly subject, so she hadn't mentioned him yet. One comment from Micah, though, made her think that Isaiah had left the Amish community, as well. Only, unlike Micah, he hadn't maintained his ties with the family.

That must have been awful. Her parents had lost two children without any closure. First, her kidnapping, then Isaiah, who seemed to be lost to the family, though she wasn't quite sure why.

The kitchen door squeaked open. "I'm glad you're back," she called out. "Did you find the ice cream okay?"

Joss moved to the kitchen, then froze. Standing in the middle of the room, a pleasant smile on his face, was Kevin Hogan.

"You're dead."

He laughed softly. He looked like a businessman, not a killer. "Obviously, my death was reported prematurely. I'm quite well. As I planned."

She swallowed. Her stomach tumbled over. Now was not the time to get ill. "There was a body."

"Yes, there was. Not mine. A corpse stolen from a new gravesite. They hadn't even noticed his body is missing yet."

Finally able to move her limbs, Joss scurried back from him. "I don't know what you want from me."

He frowned, as if truly puzzled. "Of course you know. My dear wife took you from me and left me to deal with some very unhappy clients. Then she stole my client list. It's made for a few uncomfortable years for me. But she made a mistake. She settled in one place too long." He gave her a pitying glance. "I would say she wanted to give you a stable childhood. But it led me to her."

"But she didn't tell me anything about you." She scampered another step farther from him.

"Maybe that's true. But you know now, so it's all the same."

Without warning, he lunged at her. Shrieking,

she jumped away, taking a vase from the coffee table and hurling it at his head. He ducked. The fragile dish shattered against the wall. Glass scattered in all directions. It crunched under his feet as he advanced toward her.

There was nowhere else to run.

FIFTEEN

Joss wriggled and tugged, trying to get away, but Kevin Hogan was too strong for her. His hard fingers wrapped around her wrists, pinching them together, while he took a rope in his other hand and skillfully wove it around her wrists and between her hands and tied a sturdy knot. He let go of her when she was securely bound and grabbed hold of the length of rope. There would be no getting out of this, and she knew it. But that didn't stop her from trying. Crying, she yanked. He pulled her closer. She fell forward, nearly tripping over her own feet in her desperate attempt not to land against him. Instead of grabbing her, he picked up duct tape and tore off a four-inch piece. She backed away, but Kevin took hold of the hair at the nape of her neck. Holding her head still, he slapped the tape across her mouth.

"There." Satisfaction oozed from his voice.

'That should keep you quiet so we can continue in peace."

He checked her binding one last time before reaching for the hat knocked off his head during the struggle. Once it was on, he gathered the rope in one hand, and opened the door. 'This is all Emily's fault. If she hadn't gotten in my way, none of this would be happening. She could have done what I asked, and all would have been perfect. But she couldn't do that. Then she went and set the reporter on me. I was able to hire someone to break in and get this for me."

He waved the journal that had been in evidence under her nose. She fought against the despair welling inside.

"Once this journal is destroyed and you're out of the way, I'll be completely free." His voice was smooth and so reasonable, he might have been discussing the weather.

She shuddered. Her mind shifted to Calvin, still in the hospital, and Emily. Kevin had much to answer for.

He glanced around, a sneer marring his attractive features. "I can't kill you here. Too many people would look for you too soon. They'll find you and grab me long before I can make my escape." He took the end of the rope and dragged her toward the door. "There's no hope for it. I'll have to take you somewhere else to take care of you."

Shaking her head hard enough to make her long hair whip across her face, Joss dug in her heels. It was no use. There was nothing there for them to snag on to. They slid across the smooth surface like it was butter.

Kevin's strength overpowered her. Joss struggled until her energy started to fade. It really was no use. He continued to force her out the back door of her house. Had they gone out the front door, she might have been able to latch onto the railing, at least enough to slow him down.

In the end, would it have mattered? He was so much stronger.

Across the backyard, through the snow and mud, Kevin kept up a steady pace. She didn't have time to attempt an escape, she was so busy trying to stay on her feet. His longer legs ate up the distance, forcing her to nearly run to keep up. If she lost her balance and fell, she had no doubt she'd find herself dragged face down in the snow. Kevin had already told her what her fate would be.

He was going to kill her.

If only Steve were here.

Her phone. She had her phone in the pocket her cardigan. If she could somehow manage get to her phone, maybe she'd have a chance let him know where she was. She was wearg her smart watch, but her fingers were too ld to discreetly use it.

If she could even get to it. The way her hands re tied together, she didn't have the dexter- necessary to dial anyone on it. Maybe if he osened her ties, she could. She'd have to be the lookout for opportunities. If she didn't main alert, she'd die before the day was over.

Kevin shoved her in front of him. There was ar. She didn't know if this would help or hin- r her ability to escape. He opened the pas- nger door and nudged her shoulder.

"Get in."

She jerked her shoulder away from his, then oze. To her shock, he didn't react aggres- vely. Just shook his head, as if she were a ild and he was disappointed in her actions.

"You are going to get in the car," he ex- ained, his tone so gentle, chills ran down her ine. "I'm sorry it has to be this way. If Emily dn't been so selfish, you would have had a od life and never known about any of this."

The tape over her mouth prevented her from

speaking, but her eyes still worked. She narrowed them and glared at her kidnapper.

It had zero effect. He completely ignored her and jostled her closer to the vehicle until she was pressed against the open doorway. Finally he put his hands on her shoulders and applied pressure until she had to comply, and she folded herself into the seat, still glaring.

He reached down and slid his hand into her cardigan pocket, stealing her cell phone. "Can't leave this, now, can I? It would be a shame to come this far only to allow the police to track you through your phone."

He stepped away from the car and slammed the door. Walking to the front of the vehicle, he placed one hand on the hood and bent over. He stood and rubbed his hands together. Her phone was gone. She stomped her feet on the floorboard, tears spurting to her eyes. She knew what he planned.

He got behind the steering wheel and closed his door. "That takes care of that. Your phone is right up against the front tire." He confirmed her theory. "A phone won't be able to survive being run over by a car. They'll never trace you. By the time your body is found, I'll have boarded a plane at the Cleveland Airport and

e out of the country." He glanced at the time
n the dashboard. "I need to hurry, though."

He shifted the car into Drive and eased forward. A few feet forward, he peered into the
earview mirror. "Ah, perfect. Completely de-
troyed. Your friend the cop won't be able to
rack that."

Her watch on her wrist buzzed. Fortunately,
t was on vibrate mode, so there was no sound.
She knew what the notification would be. Her
phone had disconnected. Still, she knew from
xperience the watch would continue to work,
ven when her phone was off.

She just needed to access her watch. Or
maybe she could remove the tape, now that he
wasn't holding her hands captive or dragging
er, and plead for mercy.

He turned out of the driveway and onto the
oad. The same road her mother had been shot
n.

Joss deflated against the seat. If he was con-
ident enough to tell her where he was going, he
ouldn't be reasoned with. She didn't want to die.
She'd only met the Bender family. She wanted to
et to know them. She wanted to buy that puppy
he'd told Steve about. And there were so many
ifferent experiences she'd never had.

Not to mention Steve.

Joss's throat swelled. Her cop. Did he care about her? Her kiss suggested he did, even if he wasn't sold on them as a couple. If she survived, she might convince him to give them a try. But her options were slim to none.

She could jump.

Even if she died trying, she was being driven to her death anyway. At least this way, she'd go down fighting. But if she didn't die, she might be able to make a run for it. He was bigger than her, but she could fit into smaller places. All she had to do was get somewhere populated and find someone to help her.

That wouldn't be easy. She surveyed the bumpy, pothole-cluttered dirt road. She knew this road well. There weren't many homes. The closest one had burned down a little more than a year ago. Nothing had been done with it. The next house was nearly half a mile past that.

This was her best opportunity, though.

Kevin muttered. She didn't catch all the words. It was something about the horrific state of the road. He had no choice except to drive slowly or he'd wind up in a ditch or damage his car on the rough terrain. She hadn't heard the door locks engage when he'd turned onto the road. Was it possible he was moving too slow? In a mile, he'd reach an intersection and turn nto a paved road. He'd increase speed, and the oors would lock. She had to move now.

Could she outrun Kevin for that long?

She was about to find out.

She snuck a peek at him. He was totally foused on driving. Sliding her bound hands toward the door handle, she risked one final peek t him and sucked in a deep breath, saying a uiet prayer as she exhaled. It was hard to get good grip with her hands roped together. She managed to grasp the handle with her fingers nd yanked on it.

The door flew open. Joss allowed herself to umble from the opening, tucking her head and imbs in. She rolled away from the wheels.

Tires slid and brakes squealed. Kevin's car kidded to a halt, inches from a snowbank. Joss umped to her feet and leapt over the drainage itch, scampering away from the road and toward the house.

Her instincts screamed at her to get to some ind of cover. She veered away from the road nd ran to the trees. She needed a place to hide. he dove under some low-hanging branches, odging to avoid getting scratched. A heavy air of feet pounded behind her. Kevin didn't ven try to keep his position secret. He battled his way through the maze of branches and roots, yelling and swearing.

He must have followed her footprints.

She set her face and kept going. The hope leaked from her with each passing second. He was coming closer. She was no match for his size and physical strength. Still, she pushed herself to move deeper into the trees.

Her foot got tangled in an aboveground root. Joss fell. The force of the impact with the ground knocked the breath out of her. Before she could recover, Kevin was upon her. He seized her arms and lifted her from the ground.

Joss struggled. Kevin held the rope in his hand, like she was a harnessed horse on a lead rope. He was going to kill her.

He pulled the gun from his pocket and pointed it at her head. His hand shook. After all he'd done, was he nervous about shooting one more person?

A spark lit inside.

"I don't like killing people myself," he mused. "Too messy. I prefer to hire others for those kinds of jobs. But you can't be allowed to live. I need to think about this."

She expected him to head back toward the car now that he'd recaptured her.

"You've proven yourself to be more trouble

han you're worth, that's for sure. I don't have he time to deal with you. But I know exactly vhat to do."

Kevin was so calm that it made her heart ace. The blood pounded in her ears. He started valking, this time heading away from his car. Weary, she trudged along behind him, her nkle aching from her fall.

Joss had no idea how long they walked. It ould have been five minutes or thirty. Her vrists were raw from the rope. With every step, ain shot through her injured ankle. Finally, hey left the safety of the trees.

Joss peered around. She recognized the place. "he charred ruins ahead of them used to be a wo-story house that had burned down while he family was at work and school. They'd cho-en to accept the insurance money and move ather than attempt to rebuild.

"This will work." Kevin tugged her to the re-nains of the house. Very little remained other han a few fragmented boards, broken glass rom shattered windows and a large gaping hole vhere the basement had been. Kevin moved up o the edge of the hole. "Oh, this will be just vhat I need. No one will find you for a long ime. And look, you won't suffer. You'll have friend."

She glanced down and shuddered, yanking and struggling with new vigor. She'd seen little more than a rattle, but there was at least one snake down there holed up for the winter. Ohio only had three species of poisonous snakes. The timber rattlesnake was one.

Without warning, Kevin shoved her into the hole.

She tumbled to the bottom. By the time she looked up, he was gone. Headed to the airport.

Joss backed into the corner, giving the snake as much room as possible. It wasn't much. Frantically, she brought her hands to her mouth and tugged at the tape. Tears of pain blinded her. She blinked. Pain was good. It meant she was still alive. She used her teeth to pull her sleeve away from her wrist. Her watch was her only hope.

She looked in the corner of the screen and slumped, defeated. No signal.

She was out of options.

"What do you mean it wasn't Hogan's body?" Steve stared at the coroner, horror rippling through his blood, leaking down his spine. His legs felt weak. He sank into a chair.

Dave looked down and began to clean his glasses. "I'm sorry, Steve. I checked the body brought in from the car fire. The teeth were still intact. They did not match Mr. Hogan's."

Steve leapt to his feet. "He's still out there, and she's all alone."

Racing from the office, he headed to his cruiser and dialed Joss.

"This is Joss. I can't come to the phone. Leave me a message. Talk to you soon!"

He tried two more times.

Steve gritted his teeth. This was the third time he'd gotten her voice mail. Why wasn't she answering? "Joss, Steve here. Call me now, please."

He disconnected the call and stared at his phone, willing her to answer. Micah. Micah had planned on taking her to dinner. She was probably out with him. It was worth trying. Opening his contacts, he located Micah's number and dialed.

"'Lo. Micah here." The marshal didn't sound anxious.

"Micah. Hi. Listen, is Joss with you?"

There was a brief pause before Micah's distinctive voice responded. "No, she's not. We decided to eat at her house. I left her at her place and ran to get her some groceries. I'm getting ready to go to the checkout now."

"Leave them," Steve ordered. "Meet me at her house as soon as you can. I'll be there in ten."

He ended the call and hopped into his car, hitting the lights. She was in danger. He could feel it in his gut. He needed every advantage he could get. Although he skipped the siren for now. If Kevin had her, he didn't want to go in hot and warn the perp.

Stomping on the gas, he peeled out. He shaved off two minutes, arriving at Joss's house in eight minutes. Micah was already there. Steve leapt from the vehicle, leaving the engine running.

"She's not here," Micah yelled at him. "Look at this."

Steve ran over to where Micah stood. There were footprints coming from the back door. Two sets. The smaller prints were merged with longer lines, as if she'd been partially dragged.

"She didn't leave willingly." His gut clenched. He should never have let her out of his sight. Hadn't he promised to protect her?

Without a word, both men trudged through the snow, following the footprints. After what felt like an hour, but had probably only been ten minutes, they arrived at a new road where the prints vanished.

"Tire tracks," Steve announced. The man had a car hidden.

"If she has her phone on her, we can ping it,

find her location." Micah strode beside him, scanning the trees.

"We can't." Steve pointed. On the driveway, a cell phone was smashed, almost beyond recognition. Only the sparkly pink shell of what remained of her case identified it as Joss's. She couldn't have answered the phone. Beside him, Micah's ruddy complexion turned ashen. His own face probably looked the same. Steve's stomach hardened and he couldn't suck in a full breath.

The monster had the woman he'd fallen in love with.

He shoved away the distracting thoughts. He would be of no use to her if he couldn't keep his head on straight. He needed to focus.

"Wait a minute." Adrenaline shot through his veins. He bounced up on the balls of his feet. "She has a smart watch. If it's still on her, we can ping that."

"We don't have much time." Micah shifted on his feet.

"Might not need it." Steve dashed up the porch stairs and tried the front door. It was unlocked. Barging into the house, he ran to the kitchen. Joss had set her mother's cell phone in the drawer. He opened the drawer and searched. There it was. Pulling it out, he turned it on.

He recalled the sequence she'd used to open it. Emily had used the date her husband had abducted Joss.

When it opened, he found and tapped the location app. "Emily, the woman who raised Joss, had an app to track where Joss was. Joss thought she was being a helicopter parent, but she obviously had a real reason for it."

Micah stood next to him, and both men sighed when her location beeped on the app. Steve frowned. "That's just down the road. We can be there within minutes."

Internally, he worried that she wasn't moving. Just because the app tracked her location, didn't mean she was alive. If she'd been able to, she could have answered his calls on her watch. Something had prevented her from doing that. *Stop.* He couldn't let his mind go that way. They needed to get to her, now.

"Let's take my car." He ran out the door. "Micah, use the phone to navigate for me."

"Will do." Micah swung around to the passenger side and jumped in, his gaze never wavering from the phone in his hand. A grim determination had settled over the former Amish man. Steve knew the feeling. He'd do whatever he had to do, sacrifice his life if necessary, to bring Joss home.

Slamming the gear shift into Reverse, he backed down the drive. No one else was on the road. He switched to Drive and followed Micah's command to travel east. They must have been on one of the worst-cared-for roads he'd ever driven on. His entire body vibrated as they hit the edges of one pothole after another. There were too many littering the road to miss them all.

"There!" Micah pointed at what appeared to be an abandoned lot on the left. Steve didn't argue. He swerved into the unplowed driveway. If there'd been two more inches of snow, he would have been stuck.

The two men exited the car and stood, both scanning the area. His instincts told him to run and find Joss, but he knew better. Basic training said always determine if a scene was safe.

"I don't see any dangers," he murmured to Micah.

Micah nodded and shut his door—carefully. Steve followed suit, making as little sound as possible. Just in case Kevin was still there.

"You search the garage," Steve whispered. "I'll look around the wreckage."

"She's close, Steve." Micah showed him the phone. They were right on top of her.

"We'll find her," Steve promised, talking to himself as much as to the silent marshal.

They split up, Micah running to the garage. Steve picked his way through the snow and rubble to what had once been a stately house. Approaching the shell of the basement, he squinted into it.

His blood ran cold. Joss was there. Alive, yes. But not well. Her wrists were tied tightly together. He could see the rope burn on her delicate skin from his position above her. She didn't notice him. All her attention was on the rattlesnake next to her ankle.

His vision dimmed for a moment and his stomach dropped. White noise filled his head before he shook it to clear it. He couldn't let his fear of snakes stop him from doing his job. Joss was depending on him.

Steve pulled out his phone. He had no bars. They needed to go get help—fast.

All thoughts about Kevin's whereabouts fled from his mind.

The next five minutes could determine whether she lived or died. And it was up to him to make sure she lived.

SIXTEEN

"Joss!" Steve called to her in a harsh whisper. Horror filled him as the viper slithered out of sight. Nausea rolled through him. He'd told her snakes were his one phobia. Kevin Hogan couldn't have planned his vengeance better. Steve murmured a prayer, one that rose from the depths of his soul. No matter what was down there, he refused to let his fears control him. The woman he loved needed him. That was the only thing that mattered.

There's only one snake. There's only one. It didn't help. One might as well have been twenty to someone with a phobia.

"Steve." Joss speared him with her eyes. Her gaze swerved to his side as Micah dropped down beside him. Tears spilled onto her cheeks as she stared at her brother.

"Joss, where's Kevin?"

She jerked her head back to face him. She

bit her lip for a moment, those clear eyes darting to where the snake had gone and back to him. Despite her situation, she was concerned about him and his phobia.

"Steve, Kevin is leaving. He plans to fly out of the Cleveland Airport and leave the country. You have to stop him."

He knew what she was doing. She was giving him an out.

No way. He couldn't leave her, not knowing what would become of her.

"Micah."

"What?" Although his face gave nothing away, fear poured off the marshal. And no wonder. He was seeing his baby sister in danger.

"Grab me the rope in the back of my cruiser. Then go and get that slimeball. Call 911 the moment you have service. Got it?"

Micah jumped up and bolted to the cruiser.

"Steve, I've been bitten."

His stomach tightened. A thick band of fear constricted his breathing. He ignored it.

Within a minute, Micah returned, throwing the rope at Steve. He also tossed a couple of blankets on the ground. Smart thinking. "You need me?"

Steve shook his head, lowering the rope

down to Joss. "You go. She's been bitten. We have to call 911, and we can't do it from here."

He didn't need to say more. Micah raced to the vehicle and slammed it into Reverse, kicking up dust as he sped away from them. It would be another three minutes before he could call for backup.

Three minutes Joss didn't have. Already her eyes were dull.

"Joss! Grab the rope, honey. Don't pass out on me. Please, Joss. Grab the rope." Sweat poured down his back. If he could, he'd climb down to get her out. But there was no way to get him back up again. The rope wasn't long enough to attach to a tree. And he wasn't sure if it was even strong enough to hold his weight. He outweighed Joss by at least sixty pounds.

His vision blurred. He wiped his sleeve across his face. He wouldn't lose her. Not the way he'd lost his mother and sisters. "Honey, please, grab the rope."

She nodded her head and reached for it, clutching it tight.

Hope blossomed in his chest. "Yes! Good. Hold on. I'm pulling you up."

Praying, he braced himself and tugged at the rope. His muscles grew taut. He didn't dare slow down. Nor could he go too fast, or he'd yank that rope right out of her grip. *Easy does it.* Hand over hand, he reeled the rope, and the woman who owned his heart, to the surface. He laid her on one of the blankets Micah had left.

"Hi, Steve," she whispered, pain dulling her eyes.

"Joss, honey, I'm going to treat that bite, the best I can."

She frowned. "Are you going to cut my leg?"

He shrugged out of his jacket. "That's a myth. If I cut your leg, it would make it worse. I'm going to bandage your leg, and splint it. The best thing to do is keep it immobile. Don't move."

He left her briefly, scouring the surrounding area for sticks to make a solid splint. He found two that would work, and rushed back to her side, falling to his knees. Her eyes were closed. Dread clenched his heart. He couldn't breathe.

"Joss, honey, open your eyes." He was barely aware of the endearment. Right now professionalism and keeping his distance were the least of his worries. If she died—no! That wasn't an option.

Her lids fluttered before peeling open. "You're back."

Her voice was slightly slurred. He needed to move quickly.

Taking his pocketknife out, he slit the bottom of her jeans, revealing twin puncture marks. Around them, the venom affected an area approximately an inch wide in diameter. The reddened flesh appeared puffy. Yanking the first aid kit open, he sifted through it until he found the sterile bandages.

"Okay, Joss. I'm going to bandage this. I want it loose, so if it feels tight, you let me know. You understand?"

"'Kay."

She sounded tired.

His hands shook, but he worked rapidly. Once the injury was splinted, he wrapped it carefully, leaving plenty of room for it to breathe. The ambulance arrived while he was tucking in the edges. He didn't look over. The paramedics could take over as soon as they reached him. Until then, he wasn't going anywhere. Steve no longer felt the snow under his knees or the wind buffeting his jacketless body. There wasn't room for anything in his mind or his heart but Joss.

The paramedics swung into place on either side of her. Cole surveyed the splint and bandage, giving him a thumbs-up. "You did good, man. We'll take her from here."

"I'd like to ride with, if that's okay. The marshal took my car."

That wasn't the only reason, but there was no need for them to know that.

"Sure. Let's use the blanket to switch her to the stretcher." Between the three of them, they lifted her weight and carried her to the waiting stretcher, careful to avoid jostling her. The less she moved, the slower the venom would travel. Still, she groaned as her body left the ground.

"We've got you, Joss. You're going to be fine. We're taking you to the hospital."

Her eyes opened and she stared at him. "Don't leave me."

"No, Joss. I'm riding in the ambulance with you."

He was as good as his word. Aubrey, the second paramedic, opened her mouth to say something, but changed her mind. Instead, she helped Cole load the patient into the back of the emergency vehicle and secured her. Then she left Steve and Joss alone. Once the doors were closed, Steve let his head drop to his chest. He hadn't been that scared in years. Tremors racked his frame. He braced himself and used the collar of his shirt to wipe his eyes.

She would live. His Joss would live. When she groaned again, the sound pierced him like a dagger. It was his fault. Had he not gotten distracted, maybe he would have protected her better.

He needed to get away from her so he could clear his head and figure out what he should do. He couldn't do that when he was close to her. It hurt, but she was what mattered. Besides, she had her own issues to handle. Maybe once the dust settled, she wouldn't want him anymore.

They arrived at the hospital.

He leaned closer to her. "I love you, Joss. Always will."

He kissed her forehead, then leaned back. The doors swung wide, and the paramedics swarmed the ambulance and rushed Joss into the emergency room without a word to Steve. He didn't mind. Their priority was Joss. He was totally on board with that. She was his priority, too.

Steve made his way inside to wait for news. He texted the chief to let him know they'd arrived. Twenty minutes later, Micah approached and handed him a cup of hospital cafeteria coffee.

"Did you get him?"

Micah swallowed some coffee and grimaced. "Yeah, I did. He was in the airport ready to board. I booked him solid."

"Did he lawyer up?"

"You better believe he did. It doesn't matter. We have him cold. Joss's testimony will be the final nail in the case. He's going away for the rest of his life."

Steve nodded. The knot of worry in his chest unraveled a bit. No one was coming after Joss again. She could go back to her life without fear. It would be a new start for her, and he wasn't sure there was a place for him in it. Maybe that was for the best.

"Good. That's great news."

Side by side the men waited. One hour. Then two. Finally, the doctor came to see them and told Micah he could see his sister. Steve walked beside Micah. Joss was in the ICU. He could see her still form through the window. Micah stood next to her, tears on his cheeks. But there was joy in his eyes. Joss was going to make a full recovery.

It was time for him to leave.

"I love you," he whispered. Turning, he walked out down the hall and out of the hospital, leaving part of his heart behind.

I love you.

The words tunneled through the fog enveloping her mind. Joss struggled, desperate to respond. She knew that voice. Steve. Had he really just said that he loved her?

I love you, too. She fought to get the words out. Unfortunately, the weariness dragging her down was winning. Her eyelids felt like there were weights sitting on top of them. No matter how she battled to open her eyes, they wouldn't obey. Eventually, she gave up and allowed herself to drift away to sleep.

Joss had no idea how much time had passed when she became conscious of voices murmuring around her. This time, she was able to pull her eyelids open, although she didn't know how long she'd be able to keep them that way. The lethargy humming through her body was a major clue to the fact that she had some pretty strong drugs in her system. There was no pain. Only a mind-numbing exhaustion.

"She's awake."

She knew that voice. It took effort, but she managed to move her head enough to see the speaker. Kathy's face came into view above her. The impatient cop wore an unfamiliar expression. She looked concerned. Seeing the worry on the forceful woman's face, panic clawed at Joss. She remembered the snake.

Was she dying?

Her voice echoed around her. She hadn't meant to shout her question out loud.

"No, no," Kathy soothed her. "You're not dying."

Another face appeared beside Kathy. Lieutenant Nicole Quinn smiled at her, gently touching her hand. "Rest easy, Joss. You're going to be fine. You're in the hospital. In a few minutes, you'll be moved out of ICU and into a private room."

"How long?" The exhaustion tugged at her. Joss couldn't find the energy necessary to finish the sentence.

"A little over a day," Kathy responded.

Wow. She'd been out that long? Her brow furrowed. She recalled nothing about the ambulance ride, or what happened since Steve—

Had he come to see her? Was that when she heard his voice? How to ask without letting on what she really wanted to know? As much as she liked and had grown to trust the two women at her side, she was not discussing such a private matter with them. Partly out of respect for Steve. But also, because she had a strong suspicion her mind made it up.

"I don't remember..." She had to work up the energy to speak. She plowed through the sleepiness slowly overtaking her. She had to get some answers. "I was talking to Steve. Did he—"

She stopped, unable to formulate the question.

Nicole and Kathy exchanged glances above her in silent communication.

"That was over a day ago, before the ambulance arrived."

He hadn't been to see her. She stopped holding the tiredness off. He hadn't come. Which meant she'd most likely imagined everything. Because if he really loved her, he'd be here with her while she fought for her life.

She'd forgotten. She was a case he was working on, not someone who actually mattered in his life.

Her mind flashed to the kiss they'd shared. That hadn't felt like the kiss you gave someone unimportant. But he'd regretted it. So, maybe he cared. But even so, it obviously hadn't been enough.

"We should tell her—"

Nicole's voice faded as she slid back to sleep.

The next time she awoke, she was in a room by herself, an IV attached to her arm. Either meds or fluids to stave off dehydration. The fog clouding her mind had lifted. That was a relief. Joss had never liked taking strong medication. Anything that interfered with her ability to think clearly or hindered her natural inhibitions made her uncomfortable. She'd always preferred to accept the discomfort or pain rather than take narcotics. Even when she had her wisdom teeth out, she'd refused the prescription her mother had filled and took ibuprofen.

Her mother. That was an uncomfortable topic. On the one hand, Joss was grateful to Emily for saving her and raising her. In her heart, the gentle woman would always be *Mom* to her. But now she had another mother. Would Edith Bender ever feel like more than a kind stranger? Did she even want her to?

Sorrow pounced on her like a cat on an unsuspecting mouse. Joss blinked to clear her vision. She focused on the dim light coming through the window. Her stomach growled. It must be close to suppertime. Apparently, she'd been fed intravenously for the past day. Hopefully, she'd be upgraded to solid food now that she was awake.

The door squeaked open, interrupting her musings.

Joss jerked her head around, relaxing into the starched hospital pillow when she saw the familiar face of Dr. Morrow, one of the physicians she worked with. He smiled and ambled over to the bed.

"I'm glad to see you back with us, Joss." He visually assessed her, taking in the IV and the readings on the machine she was hooked to. "Chief Spencer is here. He brought in your parents—Edith and Nathan Bender, I think he said—while you were still asleep. They're in the waiting room. I thought I'd come and check before I let them in."

Joss nodded, knots in her stomach. "Sure, I'll see them."

His eyes narrowed behind his glasses, but he didn't argue. Instead, he left to retrieve them. Less than five minutes later, her birth parents and the chief were at her bedside. The doctor left them.

"Joss, are you *gut*?" Edith twisted her hands together. Joss saw the way the woman had started to reach for her but pulled back instead.

They're as nervous as I am. Joss reached out. Instantly, her hand was grasped. A single tear leaked down Edith's cheek. Her Amish mother beamed at her.

"I'm fine. Really. The police saved me."

Her parents didn't react to the quaver in her voice. Steve had saved her. Would she ever see him again?

"And you're going to stay safe." Chief Spencer entered the conversation. "Your brother Micah caught Kevin Hogan and arrested him. I doubt he'll ever get out of prison. Of course, you'll be required to testify, but that should be the end of it."

"Gladly," she ground out. "I will do whatever you need me to do to make sure he doesn't escape justice." Anger simmered in her heart. Emily was dead and her family had been through the agony of losing a child because of that man's greed. Then there was Hal and his sweet Princess. And Tim, the officer killed in the explosion. Not to mention how she and Steve had both nearly died. It floored her that one man could cause such destruction without any remorse.

"Daughter." Nathan stepped closer. "I understand your anger, but remember, vengeance belongs to *Gott*. Not us."

"I remember. And I will do my best to do what God wants." She didn't say more than that. It was enough that she'd do what was right to help others avoid the same fate.

"You'll be leaving here, soon. Where will you go? You are *welkum* to stay with us," Edith offered.

Joss squirmed. She didn't want to hurt their

feelings. "Thank you. I'd like to come and stay for a few days, soon. But I think I need to go home when I get out of here."

Her mother tilted her head and examined her. "Really? By yourself?"

She sighed. "I'm a bit of an introvert. I need some time to process all that's happened. To come to terms with it."

I need time to mourn Emily.

Edith searched her face. Then she bent and kissed her forehead. "We understand."

Maybe she really did.

"I mean it, though." Joss gripped her mother's hand tighter. "I don't want to lose you now that I found my family."

Both Edith and Nathan grinned at her. Nathan chuckled. "You won't lose us. We'll stick with you forever. You may not be Christina anymore, but you still belong to us, ain't so?"

Warmth pinged in her chest and spread through her body. She wasn't alone. It would take time, but she had a family. She could get used to that.

The door opened and a nurse entered with a tray of food. "It's dinnertime, Joss."

"We'll leave you now," Nathan declared.

"Don't worry about getting home," Chief Spencer informed her. "We'll either have someone here to drive you when the hospital says you're ready to go, or we'll get your car here."

I hope I don't have to drive my mom's car. I don't think I can ever get in it again.

Joss nodded at the chief, unwilling to cause any drama. If she had to drive it home, she'd force herself to do it. But then she'd list it for sale the first opportunity she got. She'd never forget seeing her mom's blood splattered on the door.

Shuddering, she shoved the memory deep inside.

Her parents kissed her cheek and the chief nodded at her. Soon, the room was quiet again. Left alone, Joss tried to eat, but found her appetite had fled. Her mom was gone. But it was more than that. She missed Steve. The brave sergeant had claimed her heart, then vanished.

All evening, she perked up every time footsteps approached her door, hoping Steve had come to see her. He never did. Finally, deflated, she sank back onto the bed to sleep. Knowing that he'd still find her in her dreams.

SEVENTEEN

Steve rapped on Chief Spencer's door. "You wanted to see me, Chief?"

The chief held up a finger, pointing to the receiver at his ear. Steve nodded, prepared to wait in the hall. Instead, his superior motioned for him to come in and sit before returning his attention to the phone. Steve slid into a chair, tapping his foot while his boss talked on the phone.

"I'll take care of it. Thank you."

He hung up the phone. When he rested his solemn gaze on his sergeant, alarm bells went off in Steve's head.

"That was the hospital," Chief Spencer began in his slow voice.

"What? Is Joss okay?"

Steve didn't realize he'd risen to his feet until the chief gestured for him to return to his seat.

"Relax, Sergeant Beck. Miss Graham is fine.

Better than fine, in fact. They're releasing her tomorrow."

Relief rushed through him. He sagged in his chair for a second before the reality of what the chief said hit him. "Tomorrow? Will she return to her house? Chief, she was attacked there. Plus, with everything that's happened, how will she feel safe there? Will she be secure? She doesn't have any sort of security, not really. And now, with her mother gone, or rather, the woman who raised her, she'll be by herself."

He didn't even consider that she might go stay with her Amish family. Not really. They were great people, and he had seen that she could easily learn to care for them, but to become Amish? He couldn't see it. She had been raised outside of that life for too long.

So where did that leave her? Maybe Micah?

"Sergeant Beck, why is that our concern? Miss Graham is an adult. She'll make these decisions herself. And yes, we will return her to her home."

Steve blinked. "We will?"

"Indeed. I just spoke with the hospital, as you heard, and we decided that one of my officers would bring her home, as she doesn't have a car at the hospital. I thought of asking Lieutenant Bartlett. Miss Graham seemed to trust her."

Steve was already shaking his head.

"You disagree, Sergeant Beck?" The chief's voice was smooth, but Steve wasn't fooled. He saw the smile twitching at the corner of Chief Spencer's mouth. The man knew he'd object.

"Yes, sir. I've bungled things, big-time. But I want to make it right."

"Bungled? We have caught the villains and saved the woman. What more could we do?"

Steve puffed out his cheeks and allowed the air to seep out like a leaky balloon. He'd been a fool, leaving her like he had. And he'd regretted it ever since. He hadn't felt complete since he'd rejected what they could have been.

The chief was waiting. Steve drew in a deep breath. He needed to say it. "I care for her, Chief. I—I think I actually love her, and I walked away from her, leaving her in doubt when she needed me."

"Then you need to make this right, Sergeant. This might be your only opportunity."

"Here you go, honey." A nurse rolled a wheelchair into Joss's hospital room. Although she'd never worked directly with this particular woman, she'd seen her around a few times.

Joss paused in the middle of sliding her feet into her shoes. She kept herself from rolling her eyes, but it was a struggle. She'd worked with hospitals long enough to know that no one left the hospital on their own two feet. All admitted patients were required to be escorted out in a wheelchair. After all she'd been through, being pushed around by someone she didn't know made her uncomfortable. But rules were rules. Steve and Micah had caught the bad guys, and after several days in this room, she was going home.

Steve.

She winced. He'd rescued her and then he was gone.

Did he really say he loved her? Or had she dreamed that in her venom-induced hallucination? If only he'd come to see her, she would have asked. Even if he denied it, it would have been preferable than the angst of constantly wondering. Wouldn't it?

Steve hadn't come to see her, but Chief Spencer and Kathy had.

"Has anyone shown up to drive me home? Or did they drop my car off?"

Chief Spencer had assured her he'd do one or the other. That was two days ago. Who knew if he'd remembered, though? She hadn't heard anything since then. She rejected the worry as soon as it appeared. Chief Spencer wasn't the type of leader to make empty promises or to fail to keep his word. No, he was the kind of man who instilled loyalty in all who served under him.

Someone would come.

"I haven't seen anyone yet," the nurse responded, pushing the wheelchair to the bed and setting the brakes. "We'll stop by the front desk on our way out. If your ride isn't here, I'm sure you can call someone."

Little did the nurse know that Joss had no one she could call. Other than the police. Even though she had found her family, they didn't have a phone in their house, or a car they could drive to come and get her. Well, Micah could. But she didn't know him well enough to call him up and ask him to do her a favor.

He saved your life. When you needed him, he came through.

Comforted by the thought, Joss stepped down from the hospital bed and lowered herself into the wheelchair. The nurse hummed a happy little melody under her breath as she backed up and turned the wheelchair toward the hospital door. Out in the hallway, they rolled toward the elevator.

Joss felt her breath hitch. She might never feel comfortable getting into a small space with a stranger again. The nurse patted her shoulder. "Don't like elevators do you, honey? It's all right. We'll be out of here in a jiffy."

If only she knew why her patient didn't like elevators. Even though the basement had been open, she'd been trapped and helpless, confined within the walls with no way to climb out. Just as she was in an elevator. There was no escape until the doors opened.

Joss sucked in a breath. She wouldn't let that experience keep her from living her life. God was in control, and always would be. Joss would trust in that, even when her insides quivered.

The elevator doors whooshed open, and they proceeded to the reception desk. The nurse parked her right in front of the receptionist. "Hey, Betsy. Anyone here to give Josslyn Graham a ride home yet?"

Josslyn Graham. If someone had told her one day she'd cringe at the sound of her name, she would have scoffed. Yet it was true. She was still Josslyn Graham, but at the same time, she wasn't. Not really. She was Christina Bender. And she was Joss. On all her legal documents, to those who knew her in the English world, as she was beginning to think of it, she was the same. Only she, the Bender family and the law enforcement people who'd protected her and risked their lives knew the truth.

She couldn't become Christina. Her life had taken her too far from that, but she no longer felt comfortable in her own skin with the last name Graham either. Maybe she could compromise and change her surname to Bender?

She was suddenly aware of the silence. She jerked her head up. Both the receptionist and the nurse watched her, their faces expectant. Oh. What had she missed?

She flushed. "Sorry. I wasn't paying attention."

"That's all right, Joss. I know you've had a hard time." Betsy leaned forward and smiled. "I was just saying that the chief had indicated he'd have someone here, but no one's shown up yet. Should we call?"

She bit her lip and pondered. She didn't want to be a nuisance, but neither did she want to remain here in the lobby in a wheelchair. She nodded. "Yeah. If you wouldn't mind. Please."

"Sure thing." Betsy put her headset on and dialed the phone. Joss waited, clenching her hands together to keep from fidgeting. Betsy nodded and pointed to her headset. Someone must have answered. "Yes, this is Betsy, the receptionist at Memorial Hospital. Chief Spencer was going to send someone to drive Joss-lyn Graham home. She's being released now. Sure. Here she is."

Betsy disconnected the headset and handed a cordless receiver to Joss. "The chief wants to talk with you directly."

"Oh. Thanks." She reached up and grabbed the phone. Fumbling with it for a second, she held it to her ear. "Joss here."

"Good morning, Joss," Chief Spencer's grav-elly voice greeted her. "I'm glad to hear you're being released today. I'm sorry that your ride is a bit late. It couldn't be helped. Your driver is on the way. He needed to make another stop before he got to you. But he should be there in the next five minutes or so."

"That's fine. As long as I know someone's coming. I'm not going anywhere."

"If no one arrives, let me know and I'll take care of it." A moment later, the call discon-nected.

She nodded at Betsy and handed back the phone. "I guess I'll just wait."

So, she sat. And waited. Five minutes stretched into ten. But Joss refused to call the chief back, even as she avoided Betsy's eyes.

And then the lobby doors swooshed open, bringing in a blast of freezing air—and Steve.

Her heart stopped, then kicked into a gallop. Her emotions swirled inside her. Joss didn't know if she was happy or scared, or maybe a combination of both. She devoured him with her gaze, attempting and failing to read his face and body language. Had he been ordered to come and get her, or had he volunteered? When he shifted on his feet in front of her, she realized Sergeant Steve Beck of the Sutter Springs Police Department was nervous.

"Hi, Steve." Her voice came out soft, but it was all she could manage to squeeze from her clogged throat. She swallowed to dislodge the solid mass of emotion and tears.

"Hey." He cast his eyes down before meeting her gaze. "Joss. Good to see you."

Was it?

"You didn't visit."

Oops. She hadn't intended to hurl that accusation at him. Not yet anyway.

He flinched slightly. Oh, yeah. He knew he'd done wrong. "I know. I need to get you home. And I need to explain. Will you let me? Kathy's waiting outside. If you won't go with me, she'll do it."

Out of the corner of her eye, she saw Betsy leaning forward, watching the unfolding drama without any hint of shame. Nope. Not a conversation she was having here.

"Take me home, Steve."

His shoulders sagged slightly. He smiled at her, a barely there tilt of his lips, and then he moved behind her. She felt the brake release and then he gripped the handles of the wheelchair. She leaned back.

Steve pushed the wheelchair toward the outside doors. The nurse hovered at their side, ready to reclaim the wheelchair the moment Joss was securely in a vehicle.

Pressing her lips together, Joss kept the torrent of words burning inside her at bay. Now was not the time. Steve's cruiser was waiting under the carport, engine running. Kathy leaned against the side of the car, texting. She glanced up as they approached and slipped the phone back in her pocket.

"All right then? I'll follow you."

She'll follow them? What was going on? Frowning, Joss peeked up at Steve, intent on demanding answers. His gaze, oddly pleading, silenced her. She'd wait, for now. She trusted both of these sergeants with her life. The warmth of his body heat at her back wrapped around her. Sighing, she closed her lids. For this moment, she'd enjoy his presence and go along with whatever he had planned. Even if he broke her heart, she'd have a few more minutes to savor with him before he walked out of her life.

Inside, though, hope sparked. Maybe he hadn't come to say goodbye. She remembered his voice whispering to her. Whatever else happened today, she'd finally know if her love for him was returned or if she needed to forget him and move on with her life.

When Joss removed her glare from him and focused her attention on Kathy, Steve huffed out the breath he'd been holding. For a moment, he'd been certain she'd reject him, and demand Kathy drive her home. He wouldn't have blamed her, not after the way he'd treated her. His conversation with the chief had helped him readjust his priorities.

Moving with care, he pushed the wheelchair to his cruiser, pivoting it so she could stand and move directly into the car.

He opened the vehicle door, then turned back. He'd intended to assist her, but she'd stood and hopped into the car on her own, grabbing the door panel and slamming the door behind her.

This was not going to be easy.

"You've got your work cut out for you,

Romeo," Kathy whispered. "I'm praying for you, but don't mess this up."

"I won't." He hoped. That decision remained firmly in Joss's pretty hands. He sent up a silent plea for help. He believed God had blessed him when he met Joss. Now it was up to Steve. "Do you have it?"

Kathy sauntered away, responding over her right shoulder. "I do. And you owe me, my friend. Big."

It was a debt he'd gladly repay.

Loping around the front of his cruiser, he opened the door and slid behind the wheel. He reached out and let his hand hover over the temperature controls. "Warm enough?"

Quit stalling, Beck.

"It's fine. I'm good. Let's just go."

Not a promising beginning. He drew in a deep breath as he headed toward her house. He wasn't going to have this discussion in the car. He needed to be where he could focus one hundred percent on her. Only then could he prove his sincerity.

Blood pounded in his ears during the short drive to Joss's house. Would she feel he'd overstepped? The windchill was fifteen degrees Fahrenheit. Despite the frigid January temperature and the snow coating the town like a

Rockwell landscape painting, sweat beaded his forehead and dampened his collar. He was in a fight for his heart. And he had no clue how it would all play out.

After what felt like an hour, they arrived back at Joss's home. Joss sucked in a breath as she saw the house.

"That's a new door!" She gasped.

"Yes. I couldn't let you come home feeling unsafe in your own place. I finished it this morning. That's why I was late."

Had he done too much? She still didn't know the extent of it. He opened his mouth to confess everything. Before he said a word, she shifted in her seat and her tear-filled eyes met his. He swallowed. He would happily do anything he needed to receive such a look from her.

"You fixed my door? You could have hired someone. I would have paid for it."

He shook his head. "I wanted to." He grimaced. "I'm afraid that's not all I did."

Her eyebrows lifted high on her forehead. "What else?"

"You'll see." He opened his door and jogged around to her side. He'd salted the driveway and the steps so she wouldn't fall on the path. He opened her door for her. When she rose from the car, he closed the door and swept his arm toward the steps. "We'll talk inside."

She didn't protest. When he stepped beside her and placed a steadying hand on her shoulder, she peered at him, but remained silent. His pulse raced. Silently, they climbed the stairs to the porch.

Joss's forehead scrunched. "What about Kathy?"

He peered at his colleague. She sat behind the wheel of her car, watching. When she gave him a thumbs-up followed by a shooing motion, Steve smiled. "She's waiting in her car for a few. She'll come in soon. She's giving us a little time to talk privately."

Joss's cheeks glowed pink, but she nodded.

Steve removed the new key to her door and handed it to her. Her hands shook as she unlocked the door. Due to the memories or was it his presence? Probably a mix of both.

Once inside the house, he helped her remove her coat. She moved to the kitchen and turned on the Keurig. "I'm getting coffee. Want some?"

"Maybe later. I think we should talk first." If she didn't want him to stay, the coffee would settle like a cement brick in his stomach. He waited until she was sitting across from him, a steaming mug cradled in her hands, before he began. "Joss, I've already told you about my family. What happened with my dad? How he'd basically killed my family."

She nodded, her face softening.

"I have spent my entire life since feeling like I should have found a way to prevent that."

She broke in. "You were a kid! Steve, you were no more responsible for that than I was for getting kidnapped."

He smiled at her, his heart warming at her words. "I know that, now. But my feeling of responsibility drove me to becoming a cop. And when I met you, at first, it was what drove me to protect you."

The light in her face dimmed. He hurried to explain. "Only at first. Joss, you got under my skin so fast, I couldn't fight it. I had trouble looking at your case as a cop. When you were abducted, then bitten, all I could think was that I had failed you, too. Because I had lost perspective, you were hurt."

She jumped from her seat and pulled her chair close to him so fast he blinked, startled. Her hands were warm on his. "Steve, you were amazing. I know you have a snake phobia. But you came after me, facing your worst fear. You *saved* me. I don't know how you can blame yourself for someone else's actions, especially since you see people making bad decisions everyday as a cop."

He gripped her hands, bringing them to his lips and placing a kiss on her knuckles. "I blame myself because I didn't keep my professionalism. Somewhere along the line, I went from admiring you to falling head over heels in love with you. I couldn't wrap my head around it, it happened so quickly."

"I knew I heard you say that."

Still, she hadn't said it back. Well, he had more to confess. "I know I should have asked, but I tried to tell myself that you were better without me. And yet, I couldn't stand the thought that you would come home and not be safe." He swallowed. "I had the door fixed, but it wasn't enough. You can undo it, but I also made arrangements for a security system."

She tugged her hands away, her expression flat. His heart shriveled. He had gone too far.

"So, the door and the security system... This is goodbye?"

What?

"No! I mean, I had originally thought that, but then I couldn't leave you. I love you, Joss, and yes, I need to see you safe, but I also came to my senses and realized I want you in my life.

I know I goofed, but do you think you could give me a chance? Do you think you could learn to care for me, too?"

He was nearly out of breath, he'd spoken so fast.

Then she was there, her fingers touching his cheek. "Oh, Steve. I love you, too. I thought you were rejecting me."

"Never."

It sounded like a vow. He bent and kissed her, showing her how important she was to him. Her sweet response stirred his soul. She amazed him.

A knock at the door startled them apart.

"Hello?" Kathy called out. "Someone was getting antsy."

Kathy walked into the kitchen. A German shepherd puppy waddled from behind her, his little tail wagging. He yipped and danced in place.

"Oh!" Joss dropped to her knees in front of the puppy. Immediately, he began to squirm and jump against her, his tongue licking her hands. "He's so sweet! Steve, you got me a puppy?"

He joined her on the floor. "This is Max. I know you had a fear of dogs once, so if you don't want him, I already know of a good home for him. But Max will be a good companion—"

"And a guard dog," Kathy interrupted.

Joss laughed, a tear spilling onto her cheek. "I love him. And I love you!"

She threw her arms around him and kissed him. Kathy snickered. Steve ignored his colleague. The precious woman in his arms was all that mattered. Unconcerned with their audience, Steve kissed her back while Max yipped and played around them.

He'd found the woman who completed him and would give her no reason to ever doubt his love again.

EPILOGUE

Joss squeezed her eyes shut as her mother enfolded her in a tight embrace. The sweet scent of the cinnamon rolls she'd helped Edith make for breakfast that morning clung to her mother's hair and apron. Joss inhaled deeply. She'd never smell that aroma again without thinking of family. Nathan stepped close and patted her shoulder.

"Thank you for letting me come," Joss choked.

Edith's hug eased. Her mother stepped back and touched her cheek. "You are my daughter. It doesn't matter how long you've been gone. You are always *welkum*."

Joss nodded, then turned to hug her brothers, Zeke and Gideon. It was a little awkward hugging Zeke. He wasn't as open as the others. Still, she treasured the relationship they were slowly building. Gideon, on the other hand, nearly pulled her off her feet in his enthusiasm. She gave him an extra squeeze. *I have a twin.* Would she ever get used to the wonder of it? She grinned at Gideon when he set her back on her feet.

Then she glanced around. Micah was standing by the door. He'd already put their bags in his car. He raised his eyebrows at her. "You ready to go?"

"Yeah." She gave her family one last smile and a small wave before walking out the door and into the bright late-morning sun. It was chilly for April. Pulling her coat tighter around her body, she stepped up into Micah's car, arranged herself comfortably on the heated seats and turned her cell phone back on. The battery was low. Grabbing the medium tote bag sitting at her feet, she shuffled through it until her fingers felt her charger. Once it was plugged in and her phone was charging, she slipped her arms out of the coat. Soon, she'd be home. She'd see Max. And hopefully, tonight she'd see Steve. He'd been unable to come with her due to being involved in a court case. She'd missed him, of course. The one benefit, though, was that he and Kathy had promised to take turns stopping by her place and caring for Max.

She sighed quietly, suddenly anxious to be home.

"Thanks for giving me a ride home, Micah."

Joss leaned back against the leather seat and sighed. She was exhausted, but it was a good feeling. She shifted to see her oldest brother sitting behind the wheel of the dark SUV. "I appreciate you taking the time off work. I know it was an inconvenience."

Her brother's entire life seemed to be consumed by his job. She'd been thrilled when he'd taken vacation time and spent the past three days with her and their Amish family. There was still some stiltedness between him and their parents, but it was less noticeable than before.

Micah shook his head, a half smile tipping his lips upward. "You are my sister. It is never an inconvenience." He pulled up to a red light, and turned his head, meeting her gaze. "I decided to take a look at my priorities. I failed you once and lost you. I am not going to miss out on having you in my life from now on. Whenever you need me, I will be there."

"You didn't fail me, Micah. You were only a kid."

He shrugged.

"You're a good man, Micah Bender. I'm happy you're my brother."

This time, he grinned at her. "Back atcha, sis."

The light changed. Micah refocused on the drive. She'd never seen anyone so focused while driving. Not that it was a bad thing. She knew he had a perfect driving record.

Her mind drifted over the past weekend. She'd been so nervous about spending so much time with the Bender family. The last time she had been in their house, she'd been on the run, scared for her life. But the weekend had passed quickly, and she had grown comfortable with them. Part of her had feared there'd be some pressure to rejoin the community she'd been torn from more than two decades earlier. Her parents, however, were pleased to accept her as she was. After growing up with only her mom, meeting the large Bender family had been somewhat intimidating. Well, meeting most of them.

"Do you think I'll ever meet Isaiah?" It wasn't a question she'd ask anyone except Micah. She'd met the entire family this visit except him. Micah had told her before they'd arrived at the family home not to mention him to their parents. Isaiah's refusal to have anything to do with his Amish roots was a sensitive subject.

Micah huffed a sigh. "I don't know. I'd like to think so, but I doubt it. He left the first opportunity he got." He drummed his fingers on the steering wheel. "I found him once and tried to reconnect, but there was no response."

Joss let the subject drop, but she wasn't giving up. She'd continue to pray for Isaiah, just as she prayed for her parents, Micah, Zeke and Gideon. And Steve. They passed the Plain and Simple Bed-and-Breakfast. Home was only five minutes away. Soon she'd see him.

Joy blossomed in her chest and spread through her entire body. She couldn't stop the smile blooming on her lips.

"Uh-oh. Thinking about the boyfriend again, am I right?" Micah winked, smirking.

Heat flooded her face. She shrugged. She couldn't help it. Leaning forward, she took her phone and sent Steve a quick text.

Home in 5.

Her eyes stayed glued on the phone until it chirped.

See u soon.

Satisfied, she smiled and relaxed. Five minutes. She could wait that long. Or maybe a little longer. If he was at his apartment, he'd get there ten minutes after her. Enough time for her to put her bags away and run a comb through her hair. Not enough time to put makeup on, not that she planned on it. Running for her life had gotten her out of the habit of wearing many cosmetics.

Micah turned onto her driveway. "I'm glad you decided to stay in Sutter Springs."

Joss watched the familiar landscape pass. The trees were in full bloom. Soon, apples and pears would fill the fruit trees in the backyard. She'd enjoy picking them. Maybe she'd ask her mother to teach her how to make apple butter and jam this year. "I was tempted to sell the house. So much had happened. But with the new security system in place, and Max, I decided to stay. This is my home."

She would have said more, but they rounded the final curve and arrived at the back of the house. Steve was here! Her heartbeat kicked up. Micah parked next to Steve's truck. "I can't believe he's here! I didn't know what time I'd be home."

Micah grinned. "Huh. I wonder how he knew?"

"Micah Bender! Did you tell him?"

She recalled him being adamant that he needed to get the bags to the car before she said goodbye to the family. She'd assumed he was giving her time to say farewell privately, but now she narrowed her eyes at her smirking older sibling. Micah didn't respond. Instead, he opened his door and hopped out. The front door opened, and Joss's gaze shot in that direction in time to see the man she loved stride out of her house and tromp down the steps, Max frolicking at his side. By the time she was out, Micah had her bag and was giving it over to Steve. The two men shook hands.

"Thanks, man," Steve said.

Thanks? Thanks for what?

"No problem." Micah swooped down and hugged her, planting a kiss on her cheek. "See you later, sis. Text me or call anytime."

"I will." She watched him open his door again. "Micah!"

He turned his head to look over his shoulder. "Yeah?"

"Love you."

He winked, his expression soft. "Love you too, Josslyn."

Steve shifted her bag to his other hand and looped his arm around her shoulders, pulling her close to his side. She leaned into him. Together, they watched Micah pull down the long, winding driveway until the blossoming trees hid his vehicle from view.

Joss lifted her face to the handsome man looking down at her with so much love that her breath caught in her throat. He leaned down and kissed her gently.

"Welcome home. I missed you."

Max got tired of waiting and butted up against her. Laughing, she bent over and scratched him behind the ears, getting a doggy kiss in return. "Yuck. I think you both missed me."

His deep chuckle warmed her. Linking their hands, she started for the house. "I was shocked to see your car here. I had no idea my brother had told you we were coming. Have you been here long?"

He pulled the screen door open and gestured for her to proceed him into the house. "Long enough."

She quirked an eyebrow at him and headed for the kitchen. "What does that mean? Long enough for—"

Her mouth dropped open. Not at the large vase filled with roses resting on the kitchen table. Not even at the streamers floating from the ceiling. It was the banner stretching across the cabinets over the counter that caught her attention.

MARRY ME, JOSS

Whirling to face Steve, her eyes dropped to find him on one knee in front of her, a glittering diamond engagement ring pinched between his fingers.

"Josslyn, I know we haven't known each other that long, but I love you, and I don't want to waste any more time. I want to spend my life making you happy. Will you marry me?"

She dropped down on her knees beside him, tears clouding her vision. "Oh, Steve! Yes! I love you, too. So much."

Trembling, she held out her hand. He gently slid the ring on her finger. Lifting her hand, he kissed her fingers. She shivered.

"You're right, we haven't known each other long. But I can't imagine my life without you."

He slipped his arms around her and slowly kissed her until a wiggly puppy decided he needed some attention, as well. Laughing, they broke apart and stood. Joss couldn't stop grinning. She had everything. Family. Friends. And a man who adored her. God had blessed them beyond what she had ever thought possible.

Life with Steve would be an adventure. She couldn't wait to see what the future held for them.

* * * * *

*If you enjoyed this book, don't miss the other
heart-stopping Amish adventures from
Dana R. Lynn's Amish Country Justice series:*

*Available now from Love Inspired Suspense!
Find more great reads at
www.LoveInspired.com.*

Dear Reader,

I love revisiting characters from previous books! There are so many possibilities. When I began writing this story, I started with Micah Bender's story. A couple of chapters in, I realized I couldn't tell his story until I told his sister's, as her story is his backstory. I started again with a new plot and new characters.

Sergeant Steve Beck was first introduced in *Amish Cradle Conspiracy*. He was not meant to be a main character, but something about him intrigued me. He had so much more depth and pain inside but was still so strong. Joss Graham's entire life is a lie, but she has the grit to handle it.

I love hearing from readers! You can contact me on my website, www.danarlynn.com. If you want to keep up with my writing news, feel free to sign up for my monthly newsletter.

Blessings,
Dana R. Lynn

Get 4 FREE REWARDS!

We'll send you 2 FREE Books plus 2 FREE Mystery Gifts.

Both the **Love Inspired®** and **Love Inspired® Suspense** series feature compelling novels filled with inspirational romance, faith, forgiveness and hope.

YES! Please send me 2 FREE novels from the Love Inspired or Love Inspired Suspense series and my 2 FREE gifts (gifts are worth about $10 retail). After receiving them, if I don't wish to receive any more books, I can return the shipping statement marked "cancel." If I don't cancel, I will receive 6 brand-new Love Inspired Larger-Print books or Love Inspired Suspense Larger-Print books every month and be billed just $6.49 each in the U.S. or $6.74 each in Canada. That is a savings of at least 16% off the cover price. It's quite a bargain! Shipping and handling is just 50¢ per book in the U.S. and $1.25 per book in Canada.* I understand that accepting the 2 free books and gifts places me under no obligation to buy anything. I can always return a shipment and cancel at any time by calling the number below. The free books and gifts are mine to keep no matter what I decide.

Choose one: ☐ **Love Inspired
Larger-Print**
(122/322 IDN GRHK)

☐ **Love Inspired Suspense
Larger-Print**
(107/307 IDN GRHK)

Name (please print)

Address   Apt. #

City   State/Province   Zip/Postal Code

Email: Please check this box ☐ if you would like to receive newsletters and promotional emails from Harlequin Enterprises ULC and its affiliates. You can unsubscribe anytime.

Mail to the **Harlequin Reader Service:**
IN U.S.A.: P.O. Box 1341, Buffalo, NY 14240-8531
IN CANADA: P.O. Box 603, Fort Erie, Ontario L2A 5X3

Want to try 2 free books from another series? Call 1-800-873-8635 or visit www.ReaderService.com.

THE 2022 LOVE INSPIRED CHRISTMAS COLLECTION

Buy 3 and get 1 FREE!

May all that is beautiful, meaningful and brings you joy be yours this holiday season...including this fun-filled collection featuring 24 Christmas stories. From tender holiday romances to Christmas Eve suspense, this collection has it all.

YES! Please send me the **2022 LOVE INSPIRED CHRISTMAS COLLECTION** in Larger Print! This collection begins with ONE FREE book and 2 FREE gifts in the first shipment. Along with my FREE book, I'll get another 3 Larger Print books! If I do not cancel, I will continue to receive four books a month for five more months. Each shipment will contain another FREE gift. I'll pay just $23.97 U.S./$26.97 CAN., plus $1.99 U.S./$4.99 CAN. for shipping and handling per shipment.* I understand that accepting the free books and gifts places me under no obligation to buy anything. I can always return a shipment and cancel at any time. My free books and gifts are mine to keep no matter what I decide.

☐ 298 HCK 0958   ☐ 498 HCK 0958

Name (please print)

Address   Apt. #

City   State/Province   Zip/Postal Code

Mail to the Harlequin Reader Service:
IN U.S.A.: P.O. Box 1341, Buffalo, NY 14240-8531
IN CANADA: P.O. Box 603, Fort Erie, ON L2A 5X3